Insights

"Well, I guess I'd better go home," Tess said, but she didn't move. She liked the feel of Forrest's hand, wanted it as she'd wanted no touch since Bill's. She swallowed, and Forrest's arm eased around her shoulder. He shifted closer, and she raised her mouth to his.

She touched his cheek, marveling at his gentleness. The movement of his hands excited her. He tipped her head back, stretching her body straighter before him. She opened her mouth to him as his hand moved up to brush her breast.

It's right, she thought thickly. There's something completely right about the two of us. I want that completeness. I want to wake up in his arms.

Then, as though hit with a sheet of ice, she remembered Zach.

Abruptly and with shaking hands, she pushed away. How could she be sitting here, feeling . . . this?

Also by Mary Ruth Myers
Published by Ballantine Books:

A PRIVATE MATTER

Mary Ruth Myers
is an ex-journalist living in Yellow Springs, Ohio and
the author of several novels including a sweeping histori-
cal romance, *Captain's Pleasure*, (Fawcett, March '81).

Mary Ruth Myers

Insights

BALLANTINE BOOKS • NEW YORK

Library of Congress Catalog Card Number: 82-90919

ISBN 0-345-30966-9

Manufactured in the United States of America

First Edition: May 1983

For Mom and Dad Myers

Chapter One

"ARE YOU A STAR, MOM? LIZ ELLIOT SAYS YOU HAVE to be a star to have your own TV show.''

As they stopped in the driveway, Tess Bondurant reached across the car seat and rumpled her son's sandy hair.

"Oh, Zach. You loon! Of course not,'' she said, laughing. Only a nine-year-old could suppose a job that barely paid the bills, at a still-struggling station in Springfield, Ohio, population 75,000, qualified one for any kind of fame. Nevertheless, she loved him for his loyalty, just as she loved the job that had been so hard won.

Zach grinned back at her, and she saw the mirror image of her own face: freckled nose, ruddy cheeks, bright blue eyes always ready to tease. Features better suited to blue jeans than to polished fashion, she thought. Zach's father had always wanted—but that didn't matter.

"I told her you weren't,'' Zach said as he hauled a red kite out of the seat beside him. "But you know Liz. D-U-M-B. Yeah, yeah,'' he added with the haste of one who'd heard a lecture too many times. "Girls are just as good as boys, I know. But ugh!''

Tess laughed again, slamming the car door, and they walked together toward their ranch-style house, an empty picnic basket swinging between them. They had shared a lot of laughter today, skipping church (as Tess sometimes worried they did too often) to launch their homemade kite in a gusty March sky.

1

"Boy, I bet dad'll be impressed when we tell him how high this thing flew," said Zach, as though his thoughts, too, had returned to those lazy hours.

"I'll bet," Tess echoed. Zach's father probably wouldn't give a damn, but in the two years since their divorce, she'd taken pains not to say or do anything that would tarnish his image in his son's eyes.

"Would you take the kite in? Can I play outside till dinner time?" her son asked all in one breath.

"If you'll be home by five-thirty sharp. Tomorrow's a school day. Hey—" she called in afterthought as he bolted up the sidewalk of the cul-de-sac. "Where will you be?"

He turned and ran backward, not wasting a moment. Though Zach was getting almost as tall as her own shoulder, his face was still the face of a child, loving every second of life, every adventure.

"With the guys," he called back. "Prob'ly at the lot."

Tess nodded understanding, then watched him disappear. *So I'm a star,* she thought, a smile creeping onto her lips. A local speaker on genealogy, a female doctor, three men cooking, and similar programs in the week just ahead hardly qualified her for the big time in most people's book. But the latest ratings showed she actually was starting to draw viewers from the stations in Dayton. She tossed her keys into the air and caught them, spirits high.

In the kitchen, she checked the brisket that had been slow-baking in foil since noon, then opened the windows. She breathed deeply, understanding Zach's reluctance to see the end of this first springlike day. As she leaned on the sink, her denim shirt rolled at the elbows, a popping sound from the vacant lot where the neighborhood children played made her frown.

"I'll bet those Hughes kids are throwing firecrackers up there again," she muttered. She could feel the blood vessels in her temples tightening.

Most of the time, this neighborhood was a wonderful place for children to play, with no through traffic and the wooded lot at the end of the street for a special retreat. But kids could get carried away. How did it happen she seemed to be the only parent who strolled up to investigate their games? Was it because she was overprotective? She bent over backward trying not to make Zach into any sort of mama's boy.

She poured herself a glass of wine and carried it into the living room.

"Hi, Herman," she said to the hermit crab waving his feelers over an apple core in the large aquarium placed against one wall. She would give the occasional popping sounds from the lot another five minutes. If the older kids were putting firecrackers in bottles the way they'd been last summer when she'd intervened, Zach would know enough to come home right away.

Sinking into a Windsor chair, Tess set the wine, untouched, on a table beside her and looked around a living room whose furnishings were mostly traditional and whose predominant color was a fresh cerulean blue. Why was this the one time of week when she always felt discouraged? Why was it on Sundays she always felt so alone—wondered if her decision to leave Zach's father had been the right thing?

Not that he'd given her much choice, the way he'd flouted his liaison with Caroline, she thought. Not if she had any pride.

The phone rang. She picked it up, watching Herman the hermit crab navigate toward his tree branch.

"Tess? I've been looking over your schedule for next week. How come you're not doing a Tuesday interview with this hot-shot child psychiatrist Diadazzio?" a voice demanded.

Tess recognized Josh Jergens, news director of Channel 31.

"Dr. Diadazzio doesn't give interviews. I've tried his New York office and the publicity chairman of the group that's sponsoring his speech here. He simply refuses," she said.

"Well, it makes us look pretty lax if you ask me. Right here on our own turf—and the sort of thing that's right up your alley—"

Tess knew why Josh was being this unpleasant. A few months back, she had broken her own rule against dating anyone she worked with and had gone out with him. He'd come on very strong, and she'd turned him down flat. Ever since, he had looked for any excuse to criticize her, even though in recent weeks he had launched an affair with the station's leggy young public-service coordinator, Heather Heath.

Hanging up the phone, she shook her head and sat down again. At least those sounds from the vacant lot had stopped. The Sunday paper lay before her, open to a promo ad for Channel 31 and "Tess and Guests." She surveyed it critically.

A photo showed her with light hair fluffing casually above the collar of the striped shirt she sometimes wore on the show, looking less like the star Liz Elliot thought her than the hybrid she actually was: half thirty-one-year-old homemaker and mother, half woman on her own. Like a lot of my viewers, she thought and grimaced. She wondered how many of them were lonely but seemed to meet only men of the Josh Jergens type.

In the distance, a siren was wailing, growing closer. Tess looked up uneasily, wondering when it had started, remembering that popping up at the lot. The siren sounded very close now. Just outside. Jumping up, she hurried toward the door.

Through the living-room window, she glimpsed an ambulance pulling to the curb, its red light flashing. Fear rooting inside her, she jerked the door wide, then fell back a step. A man in a uniform stood before her. A policeman. Grim-faced.

"Mrs. Bondurant?"

She could only nod.

"Has your son come home, Mrs. Bondurant? I need to see him."

The fear traveled to her midsection. Tess was trembling. In the living room behind her, distant and ominous, she heard her telephone begin to ring.

"Zach—" Her voice was a whisper of unspeakable dread. "What's happened to Zach?"

The back door banged open. Tess heard footsteps, a small voice.

"Mom?"

Dizzy with relief, she turned. Her son was safe.

Then she saw him, and a strangled sound such as an animal might make lodged in her throat. His freckled face was white and pinched. His hands, held carefully before him as though to keep from smearing anything, were covered with blood. Tess felt her insides draining out of her. She knew if she tried to move, her knees would collapse.

"Zach!" She screamed his name in spite of herself. "Zach! What have you done to yourself? What's happened?"

The policeman spoke with kindness—she would always remember his kindness.

"I'm sorry, Mrs. Bondurant. There's been an accident. One of the children up the street brought a gun out. The kids have been playing with it all afternoon, it seems. When Zach's turn came—well, we're not sure what happened. The gun went off. Andy Rowe is dead."

Chapter Two

LIGHTS. PEOPLE. VOICES. THEY SWIRLED AROUND TESS as she held Zach tight against her; trying subconsciously, she supposed, to protect them both.

At some point since this nightmare began, she had taken her son into the bathroom and washed his hands of his playmate's blood. When Zach saw Andy was injured, he'd dragged him down to the nearest house for help, someone had told her. She knew—she and Zach both knew—that removing this visible sign would in no way reduce the horror of what had happened. She held Zach more fiercely. The child who had laughed and run with a red kite that afternoon was now almost catatonic—had been even before the doctor arrived and gave them both something.

Suddenly, Tess wanted to cry. She wasn't sure she could hold up under much more of this. Everyone was being so kind: the policeman who spoke with careful politeness, the doctor who had made a house call. Yet the horror just unfolding was for her and Zach alone, wasn't it? And for the dead boy's family, she thought bleakly.

"How's Mrs. Rowe? How's her husband?" she asked the policeman, who had been making notes based on things she and Zach had told him. How many men in uniforms had she talked to already tonight? She was feeling numb.

The officer shifted uncomfortably. Before he could answer, the front door slammed open and a slender, dark-haired man strode quickly in.

Tess's heart gave a feeble leap. Zach's father was here. Maybe he would take over, ease this horror back a little.

He was an unusually handsome man, Bill Bondurant was. She watched his well-molded head swing from side to side as he walked toward them, as though by that gesture he informed everyone in the room he now was in charge.

"Tess, what the hell is going on here?" he snapped in greeting. His brusqueness where she'd hoped for support was the last straw. Tess felt tears slide out and start down her cheek.

"Bill," she said raggedly, patiently, "I *told* you what was going on when I called—"

"I mean I want to know how this happened! Why the hell weren't you keeping some sort of eye on him? On what he was doing?" He glanced at his son for the first time now. "For chrissake, Zachary! How could you do such a thing?"

Tess felt her son shrink against her, saw his face quiver.

"Shut up! It was an accident. I told you that. There's no need to make Zach feel—"

"There's a need for someone to take over here, that's clear enough," Bill cut in coldly. "I don't see your lawyer. I don't suppose you've even bothered calling him, have you? A damn good thing mine's on his way."

Stop it! What kind of father are you? Can't you love him a little—reassure him a little? Tess wanted to shout. It was miserably like all those arguments in the last rocky year of their marriage.

"Lawyer? Why on earth do we need a lawyer?" she asked.

"It would be handy in the event they sue—or hadn't you thought of that? They could try to nail us for every cent we've got between us."

Tess felt frustration and explosive anger. How could he

be so insensitive? Here was one more thing to frighten Zach.

She spoke calmly, her hands steady where they touched her child, though she shook with fury.

"I'm sure there's no chance of a lawsuit. As I keep attempting to get across to you, it was an accident."

She bent and kissed Zach's forehead, though when he'd started fourth grade, she'd promised not to do that in public again.

"Come on. Your father can deal with things out here for a while," she said in a tight voice. "Let's put you to bed."

Taking him by the shoulder, she steered him into a room with Charlie Brown characters on the walls and closed the door. Someone might very well come along and drag them out for more questions, but she'd had to get Zach away from that constant battering.

"You okay, fella?" she asked, sitting on the bed and drawing him down beside her.

The eyes that stared back at her were as dull and expressionless as two poker chips. Nearly ripped in two by anguish, Tess caught his chin in her hand and smoothed back his hair.

"Oh, Zach—baby—listen to me! I know you feel awful, but what happened wasn't your fault. The policeman says so—the guys who were with you and Andy say so. Andy grabbed in to take the gun from you, only he was standing in front of you, and—and he made it go off—"

Tess choked. She had been so glad—so desperately glad—to learn that was how it had happened. But if only she'd followed her instinct, gone to check—

"Andy's dead. And I was holding the gun," said Zach in a flat voice.

Biting her lip, Tess held him against her, fighting off waves of despair. She was trying to reassure herself as well as Zach, she realized fuzzily. But she couldn't expect to reason with him tonight. The events were too fresh in his mind. Too ugly. Tomorrow would be soon enough to try and help him understand.

Tomorrow. God, I'll have to call the studio and tell them to arrange a replacement for me.

She cringed at the thought of facing the station manager, who had hired her with reluctance, making clear his belief that women with children had too many emotional distractions to make them suitably professional in the work place.

"Let me help you into your pj's," she told Zach softly. "You can stay in here and read until all those people leave."

When she returned, Bill beckoned to her from the kitchen. She was glad to avoid the policemen, the father of one of the boys in the incident who kept flashing her harsh looks, even the kind neighbor lady from three streets over who'd come offering help.

"Zach could use you in his corner just now," she said, sagging against the kitchen counter and placing her head in her hands. "He's terrified. He didn't need you pouncing on him as if you think he's a—some sort of murderer."

"If no one calls him that, he'll be damn lucky," her former husband said darkly. "Don't you suppose I'm upset, too?"

Now she felt guilty. Of course he was distressed, and scared, just as she was. But they were the adults, the ones who should shelter Zach when he needed it, weren't they?

"Now will you kindly tell me how this all happened?" Bill demanded.

She gave him the details as best she could.

"The others had been out there several hours," she concluded. "With a box of ammunition. Shooting at cans. And *no one* checked! Damn it, I don't see why it had to be Zach who—"

She couldn't continue. Almost reluctantly, Bill reached into his pocket and offered a neatly pressed handkerchief. He wasn't a bad man, Tess thought. Just not right for her.

"I think the two of you had better go away for a while," he said. "A month or so. I'll pay for it."

That almost made her smile. Bill's child-support payments were usually late or missing altogether. No matter how large his salary, his expenses always outpaced it.

In a fleeting way, the thought of a trip had already presented itself to her. She shook her head.

"I can't just yank Zach out of school. I'm not sure it would be the best thing for him, anyway—no friends to play with, nothing to do to take his mind off what's happened—"

"And of course there's your job to consider," he interrupted, his words now edged with sarcasm.

Tess stared at him. Her every concern had been for Zach and nothing else.

"I'd give up my job right now if I thought that would help," she said, voice low and tremulous. She heard the old criticism of this particular job—the first she'd ever taken because it interested her rather than because it was strictly necessary to keep the wolf from the door.

She'd spent a lot of time fighting the wolf in those years with Bill. She thought back to the piecemeal work: waiting tables, clerking in a discount shoe store, anything to help as Bill pursued his career as an aeronautical engineer. He had left civil service because it didn't pay enough, a West Coast firm because it didn't promote him as quickly as he thought he deserved, McDonnell Douglas because of differences with a supervisor.

"What Zach really needs is to spend a few days with you," she said before the memories could turn bitter. "You're his idol. He needs to know you're not down on him."

"For chrissake, Tess. You know I can't right now. I'm in the middle of a major project!"

Bill was always in the middle of a major project. Fighting anger, Tess wondered if they'd ever really seen each other in eight years of marriage.

"How could I forget?" she said. "I think that policeman out there wants something."

She made a quick departure, scraping off tears against

the rough denim of the sleeves she'd turned down, hoping no one would see. How could she even think of finding the right man someday, knowing what a colossal mistake she'd made in choosing Bill?

As she was answering a few final questions from the police, Bill's lawyer arrived. In the midst of their short but tedious conversation everyone began to leave. The good news was the official word that this would be classified as an accident. No charges whatsoever would be filed. Finally, the front door closed for the last time, and Tess found herself alone.

She walked immediately into Zach's bedroom. He looked so small lying there face downward, almost buried beneath his blue bedspread.

"Want a glass of milk and something to munch?" she asked, sitting beside him. She knew without question that neither of them wanted real food.

He didn't answer. His child's face was a study in agony. At last, with a shake of the head, he turned into the pillow.

"Have to take one of these if you want to call it a night, then." Tess fished in her pocket for the vial of sleeping pills that had been left with her. "Doctor's orders."

Rebellion hovered briefly in his expression, and Tess held her breath. Zach always resisted, always questioned, but now he stretched out his hand with a bleak indifference that wrenched at her heart.

She caught him to her fiercely.

"Zach, it's going to be all right!" she said. But her throat ached, wondering whether anything would ever be all right again.

After he had swallowed the pill, she continued to sit with him, softly humming an old song she'd made up for him in his baby days and holding his head in the crook of her arm, waiting until his shallow breath gave way to sounds of sleep.

Would everything be all right, she wondered again, looking down at his rumpled hair? What would a tragedy of this magnitude do to Zach? Tonight, he no doubt was in

11

shock, but what if it worsened? Closing her burning eyes, she tried not to cry.

Like a hot iron searing her, she felt the desire for someone to share this lonely, frightened time with her. *Face it, Tess, you've been lonely and frightened a lot of the time, pretending to be braver than you are. It's just that this has brought it all to the surface.*

Not that she wanted a Sir Galahad to come along and sweep away all her troubles. If only there were someone to sit here with her, to touch her, to let her know that no matter what happened, she and her child were accepted—and loved.

It was what every woman probably wanted and very few found, she thought wearily. Then she steeled herself for the next task at hand.

Even after she'd walked into the living room, it took several minutes of standing by the telephone before she could bring herself to lift it and call Earle Lewis. The station manager had shown reservations over hiring her as a lowly production assistant five years ago, had shown even more reluctance when the woman who had the station's floundering homemaker show retired and it became clear that Tess, who by then had graduated to doing "soft" features for the morning news, was the logical heir.

Well, I don't care if I am reinforcing all your stereotypes. My child needs me, she told him silently. *If that makes me less than professional in your eyes, so be it. Frankly, I think the world might be in better shape if people were a little more concerned about other people than they are with getting ahead.*

"Earle? It's Tess," she said.

And she told him, as briefly and calmly as possible, what had happened to Zach.

"So I obviously don't think I should come to work tomorrow," she concluded. "P. T. ought to be able to step in pretty easily. She's worked behind the scenes on the show long enough, and she knows how to prep a guest."

There. After more than a year and a half—after carrying on through the flu, a throat infection that had made each word sheer agony, and the other assorted ills of day-to-day life—she was finally telling him she'd have to miss a day.

"I understand," he said with a lightness that chilled her. "In fact, I'm surprised there hasn't been some problem before this, what with your being a single parent. And in view of something of this magnitude, well, we'll see what happens. I've been thinking we should give Heather a try in your slot, anyway."

He hung up the phone, and Tess stood chewing her lip. Had he been threatening her? Was he hinting she might be eased out of her job because of this?

Surely not. She had friends at the station. And Earle must know she was financially dependent on that job.

There was no point dwelling on it in any case. What mattered now was Zach and moving doggedly onward just for tonight. That, she supposed, was the whole secret of survival. Anything could be faced if approached one night at a time. When you made yourself that promise, the next day almost always dawned brighter.

Getting up, Tess locked the doors and prayed it would be so.

Chapter Three

I T WAS THREE-FIFTEEN MONDAY AFTERNOON. TESS PACED and looked out the window again, her stomach churning. What ever had made Zach do what he'd done this morning, and whenever would he return? Surely it was time children should be trickling home from school.

She'd thought Zach would be relieved when he got up to find her there instead of Whitmore, the neighbor-woman Tess paid to come in five days a week and care for him while she worked. He'd watched like a small owl when she'd told him they'd had a hard night and he could stay home today. Then, when she'd been in the shower, he'd called out to her:

" 'By, Mom. I'm going to school. See you."

Flinging a robe around her, Tess had tried to catch him, but by the time she'd reached the front door, he was already almost out of sight. At least she'd called and knew he'd really gone to school. That ought to comfort her. But the day alone and the news reports she'd listened to had been sheer torture.

It was her idle nervousness that had kept her flipping from station to station. That and some vague feeling that by hearing the worst she would have to face, she would somehow be prepared for it. The shooting had been every Springfield station's lead story, tastefully treated on TV and most of the radio stations. In her mind, though, she kept hearing the one exception, and she felt again that combination of anger and despair that it had produced.

The station responsible lived always on the thin edge of sensationalism, and every detail that could conceivably be unearthed had been thrown in.

"So at the end of a day which held the promise of spring," a voice had crooned, "nine-year-old Andy Rowe, who collected comic books and was the neighborhood PAC-MAN champ, lay dead. Police have ruled the shooting an accident and say no charges will be filed against the nine-year-old son of a Channel 31 talk-show hostess—"

She'd snapped off the radio.

Now, grinding her fist against the side of the window, Tess leaned against it. How could they have all but named Zach? Why didn't anyone point a finger at the child who had brought the gun out in the first place? She looked at the telephone. Another agony of this day had been wondering if she should call the Rowes and try to voice her horror over what had happened. But how could she, of all people, intrude on them? It might be the cruelest gesture she could make.

On top of everything else, she'd watched Heather Heath take her place on "Tess and Guests." Not P. T., her friend and assistant, but Heather, nine years her junior, with long brown curls and liquid brown eyes, looking as polished as though she'd done the show all her life.

Tess sighed. At last, the children were starting to come home from school.

Most of the familiar faces were well past, and she was starting to panic when she saw him. Zach walked alone, steps slow and shoulders hunched downward, abandoned.

Tess could not bear the picture of misery that he radiated. She opened the door and went down the front walk to meet him.

"Hi, fella," she said quietly.

He looked up, but she had the same sense she'd had the night before of his eyes not seeing anything.

"Hi," he said.

They walked into the house in silence. *Give him a few minutes*, she admonished herself. *Don't pounce on him first thing, asking why he did what he did.*

"How're you doing?" she asked instead.

"Fine." The word was toneless. He set a red arithmetic book on the table with uncommon care.

"Want some brownies and milk? I baked today."

"No, thanks."

He was starting for his room, making no attempt at his usual greeting to the hermit crab, sharing nothing of what must have been a ghastly day.

"Zach, what on earth possessed you to go to school?" The words burst from her. In the archway to the bedrooms, Zach turned with the expression of a puppy hit so many times it made no protest.

"I just had to," he said. His eyes pleaded with her to understand.

"Zach, please come here. Let's talk about this, can't we?"

He obeyed, an automaton without Zach's spirit.

Tess sat on the couch, turning to rest one elbow on the back as she looked down at him. The somberness of the small face beside her tore at her heart. She touched his freckled cheek, then smoothed his hair.

"It's terrible, what's happened, Zach. But we've got each other. We've always got each other, no matter what. I don't want you to try to—to try and punish yourself, if that's what you were doing. You weren't the one responsible for Andy's death."

He didn't answer.

"Did the kids give you a bad time at school?"

He shrugged.

Now that was a stupid question, Tess scolded herself. *He came dragging home all alone. You know something must have happened.*

"I had to go," he repeated in muffled tones. "I didn't want everybody to think I was really bad."

Tess blinked back tears. She had to be strong for his sake.

"People may say mean things to you for a while—to both of us—but the important thing is that you know you're not bad. And Zach. You—we—it isn't right to think about what happened to Andy every minute. Of course it's going to hurt. It's going to hurt a lot. And we'll always remember it. But we've got to go on—do some normal things—" The right words eluded her.

He looked at her.

"If that's so, how come you didn't go to work today? Were you ashamed of me? Or wouldn't they let you work after what I did?"

"Oh, Zach! My poor little loon!" She wrapped her arms around him. "Of course that's not the reason. I just wanted to be here with you!"

Did he believe her? She didn't know. But with a heavy heart Tess realized that if she wanted to help her son, she might have to go to the station tomorrow.

She tried again at bedtime, after they had sat snuggled together with her reading part of a long book about a dog searching valiantly for its master. Zach himself was perfectly capable of reading it, but her help and the sharing seemed in order tonight.

"Look, Zach, I know you felt you had to go to school today, but—well, you've done it. I think it would be good for us to take a trip for a few days now. It might help us feel—less sad."

His mouth firmed into a hard little line.

"I want to stay here. I want you to go to work like you always do."

Was it a plea? Was it a desperate cry for the security of the normal rhythms of their lives? If it was, Tess recognized reluctantly, she couldn't afford to ignore it.

In the end, she compromised. She would let someone else—probably Heather—do her morning feature, but she would be there in time to do "Tess and Guests."

For once, when she turned into the parking lot the

following morning, her first sight of the white concrete building with blue plastic letters spelling WNNB didn't lift her spirits.

It was small, this station, and Tess knew it was the target of many a joke by their rivals in Dayton, twenty-five miles away. Even among the staff of Channel 31 itself it was waggishly said that the station's call letters stood for Wonderful No-News Broadcasts. Not true, of course, with the station's emphasis on local news, local features, proud service to a town of moderate size at best. Tess loved it for the smallness and the way tasks were juggled without the rigid divisions of larger stations; loved it for the friendliness of the people inside; loved it best of all because she, who had no real training beyond three undirected years of college and a quick mind, had found a chance and a challenge here that she wouldn't find any place else.

As she climbed the stairs to the second floor, a middle-aged black technician passed her and squeezed her shoulder.

"Hang tough, Tess," he said, his eyes voicing unspoken sympathy.

She continued up the stairs, opened a door, and slipped quietly into the control room.

A glass wall on one side overlooked the studio below where the eight o'clock news now was airing. Behind a curved desk with the WNNB logo—again in blue—floating above them sat the station's two morning anchors and Ollie, the weatherman. At the sides of the desk, within reach but safely out of camera range, sat the usual morning collection of coffee cups and half-finished sweet rolls.

The monitors on one wall of the control room showed Ollie's somber countenance predicting good weather, then cut away to Heather Heath, on location somewhere and smiling.

"Life in an all-night bakery. Pretty clever, huh, when you see your big chance opening before you but it's almost midnight. I understand she shot it Sunday night."

The voice that spoke behind Tess's ear was plainly disgusted. Turning, Tess saw Katie Blume, the only female member of the station's camera staff. She was wearing her usual working uniform of tailored slacks limp in the seat. Her normally cheerful face was dark with anger.

"Good old Josh has really hustled, as you can see, pushing his ladylove as your substitute before the body was even cold." She stopped, stricken, and the slightly distracted expression that gave her an elfin look touched her. "Oh, jeeze, Tess! I didn't mean it *that* way! I only meant—"

"I know."

Tess gave a weak grin in spite of herself, and Katie answered it. Then her eyes sparked again.

"Well, it's pretty low, if you ask me, whisking Heather into every slot of yours when poor little P. T.'s been waiting patiently for years to get her chance on camera. By the way, I really do feel for you and Zach about all this, did I say?"

"It was understood. And thanks."

They'd been whispering. Now Katie jerked her head toward the door.

"Let's go out where we can talk," she said. The man who ran the control room was an undisputed tyrant.

"I'm not surprised they put Heather on," said Tess when they reached the hallway. "She's had training for the job, which I hadn't when I started here, and she's smart."

Tess made the admission ruefully. She knew as well as Katie that the woman they were discussing had been waiting for this break ever since she'd joined the station a year ago. It was there in her smile, in the hungry glint in her eye.

"You're always so disgustingly *nice*," complained Katie. "She's smart enough not to be an out-and-out bitch so the guys catch onto her, I'll give you that. They have her scheduled for the early feature tomorrow, too. Did you know? The way Josh is praising her performance, you'd think he was launching a full-scale campaign to have her replace you—all under the guise of helping you through a difficult time, you can be sure."

Tess's insides tightened. So Heather was scheduled for the bulk of her work tomorrow, too. She was almost afraid to ask about "Tess and Guests."

"Well, screw it," said Katie, shrugging it off good-naturedly. "You've got friends a-plenty in this place. Hey, I'll bet you haven't eaten a thing this morning. I had Leroy pack an extra egg and bacon sandwich for you when he was doing mine. Come on."

"You're great." Tess felt uplifted by her friendship—the first upturn of spirits she'd felt in more than twenty-four hours.

"I know. Put my foot in my mouth rather glaringly now and then, but I make up for that by being brilliant. You're going to be surprised what jacking up your cholesterol level does for your mood."

They left the hall for what was known among the staff as the corral, a large, open room that held the desks of everyone who put together copy or appeared in front of the camera. Doors along two sides of it led to the Green Room and the offices of the station manager, the program direc-tor, and the news director. The dominant feature, howev-er, was the desks, each bearing a typewriter and lined up behind each other with all the precision of an overgrown schoolroom.

A single red rosebud in a vase was on Tess's desk. Katie's eyebrows raised.

"From Josh," said Tess, reading the card, which be-sides the name said simply, "Courage."

"Trying to look like Mr. Nice while he wedges Heather in," Katie said.

Tess didn't answer, and as she looked up, she saw Josh, in his tweed jacket, watching her from the open door of his office. His gesture with the rose puzzled her.

"So how's Zach doing?" asked Katie as they ate their sandwiches. She sat on the corner of Tess's desk, and Tess sat in the chair.

Tess shook her head. "I'm worried about him. He's all closed up—not behaving like himself at all."

"Pretty big trauma. Any help from Bill and the genteel grand-ma-ma?"

Tess smiled weakly. Bill's mother was a social leader, involved in the church council, arts council, and several other groups. She had never liked Tess.

"The only thing I've been spared so far is her hysteria."

"Speaking of hysteria, I suppose I'd better see what the assignment desk is panting to lay on me this morning. Otherwise, they'll have my head on a platter."

Katie slid away with a wave, and Tess chewed the last bit of her sandwich, surprised to discover she still had taste buds. She was glad she made it a habit to line her guests up at least two weeks in advance. Although she went through the motions of sorting the mail, she found it difficult to keep her mind on anything but Zach.

She hoped it wasn't obvious. As she greeted that morning's guest, a lady gynecologist, and led her downstairs to the studio, all seemed to be business as usual. The studio crew spoke to her casually. Dr. Chenoweth, the gynecologist, mentioned nothing about Zach's accident and instead seemed preoccupied with the worry that something she said in the course of Tess's program might be misinterpreted to the detriment of the clinic where she worked.

"If the Medical Society okayed your appearance, I'm sure they don't think there's any chance that will happen," Tess said, soothingly. Maybe very few people listened to that sleazy radio station that had all but used Zach's name.

"Women's clinics have a somewhat tarnished reputation." Dr. Chenoweth was fretting. "Ever since that woman died at the one in Columbus. But you know, women come to us who wouldn't otherwise come for medical help. And not all of them sexually promiscuous, not at all."

"Of course. That's why it's so wonderful of you to be on this show today. And that's exactly what we're going to open talking about, if you don't mind."

Her guest was looking calmer now. The tactic had

worked. Tess had learned, early on, the very real need to comfort the nervous ones. She knew they didn't see how small, local, and very easygoing this show was. To the nervous ones, this was as bad as the awesome prospect of being beamed out nationally on ''Tonight'' or ''Donahue.'' They saw only that they were putting themselves on the line, and they shared a very understandable human fear of looking foolish.

Jack, the studio production technician, as usual made a display of stepping forward and holding a white card out to check the lighting on Tess's set. Both of them knew perfectly well the lighting didn't change unless she happened to have a black guest.

''Makes 'em feel we're really in the big time, though,'' Jack had argued long ago when Tess had protested. Now he bent his head and whispered in her ear. ''Think this one'll barf?''

Only at his teasing did Tess realize she, too, was tense. She looked at him with a grateful grin for this shared joke. Scarcely a year and a half ago, during the first months of her show, an extremely uptight man whom she'd been interviewing had actually thrown up while on the air. Fortunately, the camera had switched to Tess in time, and she had somehow managed to keep things rolling. ''It could be worse—we could have another barfer'' had become the standard line for tough times among the people who five days a week put together this show.

''Thanks, Jack,'' she said with a wink. Things were almost ready now. The lights were on, and the cameras were focusing on the set of ''Tess and Guests.''

It was wedged into one corner of the studio near the news set and consisted of a yellow couch in a casual early-American style, flanked on one side by a matching chair and on the other by an end table. Behind stood a kitchen counter with a cook top recessed in it. A coffeepot sat on one of the burners, and mugs were nearby. It was a cozy set, and the theory had been that viewers would be comfortable with it—would see Tess as a friend and identify with her. Tess had always hoped no one ever learned how much she actually hated cooking.

"Now, doctor—" She touched Dr. Chenoweth's hands with one of her own, directing her attention toward the cameras, imparting reassurance, even though the station stressed never touching anyone anywhere. It was why on remotes you handed the personal mike with its small alligator clip to the person who would wear it and let that person affix it to his or her collar. Something to do with not being accused of making sexual overtures, she supposed. "Try to remember to look at the camera with the red light on," she said.

Dr. Chenoweth responded to the personal gesture as Tess had expected.

"Can do," she said with tentative cheerfulness. "I'm sorry I'm being so, well, skitterish—"

"You're fine. Absolutely fine."

Then Tess was getting the finger signals from beyond her blinding pool of light. Three seconds . . . two . . . one . . . In the last fleeting instant, she wondered how Zach was faring right now.

"Hello. Good Tuesday morning," she said, her standard opening. "I'm Tess Bondurant, and my guest today is Doctor Rosamond Chenoweth, staff gynecologist at the Springfield Women's Clinic. We're going to be talking about women's problems and women's medical services, so grab a cup of coffee and sit down with us."

There was time to sink back and draw three deep breaths while they brought up the theme music. Jack was giving her the high sign. Their start had been good.

The show went like a dream, both in the sense of no slip-ups and in the sense that Tess found she could function throughout it while scarcely thinking. Then they were into the last ten minutes and time for the phone calls.

"I was wondering where I could go for help, or if I need to," said the first one. "I have this rash that doesn't seem to go away, and it's located—um—"

"Yes, by all means get treatment," Dr. Chenoweth cut in quickly. "Come to us."

The next two, fortunately, were far more suitable for public comment. The voice of the fourth caller sounded pleasant enough, if forceful, as it began.

"I'd like to ask Tess—why aren't you home with your child after what's—"

"That's not germane," snapped Tess, too slowly and far too hotly. She cued a commercial, the fallback they'd always kept on hand for an emergency, and sat back in shock. She *should* be home with Zach—no, what she was doing was right. He wanted her to be here. He was looking to her for the cues on carrying on.

"That bitch!" growled one of the cameramen as the switch was made. "You okay, Tess?"

Beside her, Dr. Chenoweth was looking at her in perplexity.

"What on earth?"

Tess shook her head. "Let's wrap this up," she said.

The three or four phone calls that followed were mild ones.

"Thank you—and I think that woman who called and said those things to Tess was rude and cruel," the last one concluded.

Then they were off. Tess collapsed against the welcome support of the sofa back. So people knew. People who watched her knew, she thought dully. And Zach—every time he met someone, would they know about him?

She rose, saying thank yous and she didn't know what to Dr. Chenoweth. As they left the studio, P. T., the station's production assistant and all-purpose slave, came running down the stairs.

"Oh, Tess! I'm so sorry! We were monitoring, but that woman sounded friendly at first—called you Tess, and the ones who like you do that—"

"Tess!" Matt Saxton, one of the morning news anchors, broke in as he appeared at the head of the stairs and came halfway down. "Earle wants to talk to you."

Tess's stomach, already heavy with the egg and bacon sandwich, now swooped downward. Earle Lewis, the iron fist in the beachboy tan. Earle Lewis, the station manager, who could hire and fire.

Chapter Four

THE STATION MANAGER WAS A VIGOROUS-LOOKING MAN with a thick thatch of hair, which Tess suspected was white but which passed nicely for sun-lightened blond. With his tanned skin, his open-neck shirt with gold chain, and his white-toothed smile, he could have passed for a Hollywood producer who'd been misplaced.

"Sit down, Tess," he said with a broad gesture. And even though they both knew this would not be a happy chat, he remembered to smile.

Taking his place behind a large desk, he cleared his throat. Despite his attempt to keep the sound light, Tess felt nervous.

"Well, Tess," he said mildly. "That going to happen again?"

"I assume you mean that phone call." Tess's throat felt creaky. She supposed she should be decisive, bluff when she didn't know, as some of the others did, but that wasn't her style. "I can't tell you. I hope not. But I won't make promises."

Earle's mildness was worse than sitting on pins. She much preferred the tyrant from the control room, who at least let you know where you stood.

"That ten-thirty spot is supposed to be a homemaker show," he said. "It needs to stay light. Women need to trust you—"

"And because my son was involved in—in something

horrible, something which was beyond his control, you think they can't?"

"You tell me." He crossed his arms and leaned across them in a subtle statement of authority. "We don't want phone calls like the one you got this morning. It makes what should be a pleasant half hour for them uncomfortable."

Tess was shaking now, unable to believe his callousness.

"What happened to me and my child could happen to them!"

"I'm inclined to think that's the last thing of which they care to be reminded."

She stared at him. Even in her anger she could see an ugly glint of truth in what he was saying. But that was no reason to back down. That was the sort of thinking that made societies rot. Pretending bad things didn't happen didn't make them go away. Surely Earle knew that.

"You're in the public eye. That makes what's happened, though unfortunate, very different," he said in silken tones.

Tess felt a shudder. She'd felt so lucky having this job, believing she reached out to people and did some good. Now she was confronting the dark side of being a public figure.

"If there should be more calls like the one this morning, it could get to be more than a matter of your show. It could get to be a matter of bad publicity for this station. . . ."

Earle let his voice trail off. Tess gripped the arms of her chair.

"Are you telling me I'm fired?" she asked in a low voice.

"Of course not, Tess. I'm just asking if you don't think it might not be better to step down for a few days—let someone else do the show."

A nagging premonition wrapped itself around her heart. If she gave up the show, she might never get it back. Tess knew one reason she'd gotten her original production assistant's job was because the station needed to showcase a few female employees, qualified or not, and the pay had been too low to attract the former. Now it was a matter of a better job, better pay—and Heather, with a college degree in broadcasting, was waiting in the wings.

"You're giving me a choice, then?" She attempted to match his light tone. Behind his tan, she thought she detected the slight fading of his smile.

"Naturally, the choice is yours—for now."

Earle rose to show the meeting was over.

"If you like, we'll give it a few days and see how things go. Of course, Tess, I'll be rooting for you."

She had never spent much time analyzing Earle Lewis, but now Tess was certain she detected insincerity in his manner. Outside, he fell into conversation with Matt Saxton. The three of them walked together into the corral.

Heather Heath was standing by a bulletin board—suspiciously near, Tess thought. She turned at the sight of them and summoned a smile that was both warm and subdued, reaching out both hands to catch one of Tess's.

"Oh, Tess. I'm so very, very sorry about your little boy! Is he going to be all right? He must be upset."

"Yes. Very."

If Heather was piling it on, she was a more convincing actress than Earle, Tess thought. Then she felt guilty for being so unkind.

Heather's brown eyes shifted briefly to include the men in her smile. Then she appeared to concentrate on Tess.

"I know this must be a wretched time for you, and if you need some story ideas for your show, I think I have some which might work. There's this new project at the base—telepathy with dogs. I met the man who's in charge of it, and he's really a ham. He'd be great on camera. And there's a lady over in Dayton who's becoming nationally known for doing these tiny, tiny cross-stitch samplers for people who collect miniatures—you know, the really expensive ones—"

Heather looked as though she might bubble on with still more ideas, so Tess spoke quickly.

"Thanks, Heather, but fortunately I have guests lined up for the next two weeks. And the lady who does cross-stitch doesn't want to be on television. I've asked her."

"Oh, she's just a little shy. I think I could persuade her," Heather purred.

Now Tess was angry all over again. It was obvious this had been staged more for the benefit of Earle than for her.

"I did appreciate your coming in to do the morning feature for me today, though," Tess said with effort. She could be as nasty nice for an audience as Heather could.

All of a sudden, she was aware of Josh Jergens bearing down on them, his eyebrows drawn. A pipe with a curving stem hung from one corner of his mouth. He took it out and stabbed it in Tess's direction.

"I thought you told me this Dr. Diadazzio doesn't give interviews. How's it happen he was just on one of the Dayton stations?" he snapped.

Tess stared at him with a sense of being beset on all sides. Katie had been right about that rose she'd found from Josh being a guilt offering. He was doing this for Heather; doing this to make Tess look foolish in front of Earle.

With a jerky movement, she checked her watch.

"All right—if someone else got one, I'll get one," she said. She was aware of her cheeks flaming, aware of the three men watching her. "Let me see who's free with a camera. Diadazzio's due to start speaking in about ten minutes. If we really move, we can still catch the bulk of his speech and talk to him afterwards."

Twenty minutes later, Tess slipped into an auditorium filled with women, relieved that Katie had been on hand to come with her. Not only would Katie afford a welcome understanding today, they also happened to work well as a team. Katie always knew when to zoom in for a close-up, as though some instinct—or her quick perception—told her which of Tess's questions would elicit the best and most telling responses. They both were aware that one reason they were teamed together so often was the feeling of some of the male reporters that it reduced their stature to have a woman behind the camera, just as the softest features and kid stories were usually handed to Tess because she was female.

"As long as we get all the gravy and same breaks they do, I'm willing to live with their overgrown egos, and I figure you are, too," Katie had said once. Tess had laughed.

She focused her attention now on the man who was speaking. He was built like a box and kept brushing back the curly brown hair that fell on his forehead. In his enthusiasm for what he was saying, he almost bounced.

Here was an adviser any mother would trust, he spoke so positively and with such humor about how to circumvent problems, Tess thought. Goodness knows, a mother needed all the reassurance *and* all the humor she could get at times. No wonder the two books he had written had been so successful. Dr. Diadazzio projected a truly amazing warmth.

Then the questioning started, and a woman was asking how to avoid the daily battle with her two-year-old over eating breakfast. Let him feel he's choosing—does he want orange juice or cranberry juice?—the energetic man before the audience was suggesting. And something in Tess's thoughts did an abrupt about-face.

It's charming, but it's all been covered before in dozens of books, she thought. *And more than that, the questions are trifling.* "My child drags around this horrible blanket. . . ." Well, what was another year with a ratty blanket in the scheme of things? Looking around her, she felt alienated from the other women in the audience.

In a way she was one of them. She knew what it was to love a child and worry over these little things—hurdles, roadblocks, problems that left you exhausted. Yet a bitter vision had been thrust upon her. Now she knew what a real problem was.

And you don't know, she thought, looking at the row on

row of well-shod feet crossed at the ankles, the salon-fresh hair, the new spring suits. *Or maybe you do know: a child who's dying or handicapped, a child caught in a terrible tragedy like my Zach, even just the problems of raising a child alone. But no one asks questions about those things. It's not tea-and-crumpets conversation. So we avoid all those problems, and it's wrong!*

The sense of anger she'd felt in Earle's office not long ago returned to her. It wasn't right to sweep the uglier problems in the world under the rug. How many parents right here in this auditorium were suffering in isolation? Well, if she could spare just one person some of the agony she'd felt in these last two days, then she would!

"You look mighty mean," Katie whispered as the audience applauded and they rose.

Tess smiled faintly.

"Mean, huh? Well, that's not exactly the image I was hoping for."

They started for the backstage area, Katie hefting her minicam in one hand and the sound system in her other.

Dr. Albert Diadazzio stood flanked by the program chairwoman of the group that had sponsored him and a largish man whom Tess scarcely noticed. He was mopping his shining forehead with a large white handkerchief.

Tess spoke to the program lady, who looked slightly flustered at her presence, then smiled at the child-care expert.

"Dr. Diadazzio, I'm Tess Bondurant from Channel 31," she said, extending a hand. "I'd like a short interview with you for our newscast tonight."

The man who had spoken with such warmth and animation from the stage regarded her as though she were some insect unworthy of notice.

"I do not give interviews," he said shortly.

It was like being hit in the face with cold water. His personality now bore no resemblance to the one he'd projected just moments before. *The easy helpfulness and*

charm had been mere pretense, Tess thought angrily. That
and the insult of this out-and-out lie made her dig in.

"You gave one to a Dayton station," she shot back.

"Oh, Tess, I'm afraid that's my doing—and they had to
submit every question in writing ahead of time—" The
woman in charge of programs fluttered in apology.

"No interview," Dr. Diadazzio repeated brusquely, and
turned away.

He had changed into a round little stone of a man,
distant and unpleasant, a betrayal of all those mothers
who'd thought him accessible to them. Without conscious
thought, Tess's hand flew out, detaining him by the sleeve.
Hands on—very hands on, in that way you were never
supposed to be with a guest, she realized too late to stop
herself from touching him. On top of all that had happened
to her since Sunday night, this man's aloofness in the face
of the very popularity he had carved out for himself through
books and lectures laid her nerves bare.

"You *will* agree to an interview, Dr. Diadazzio—or to
be a guest on my show. Either that or I'll tell people what
an uncaring fake the real Dr. Diadazzio is! You owe it to
the women who buy your books and follow your advice to
answer some questions for them. And I'll tell you something else. You owe it to them to talk about some of the
less attractive problems—violence, handicaps, some of the
things beyond thumb sucking!"

She stopped, appalled by her outburst and realizing it
was as much in Zach's behalf as in her own that she was
making it.

Albert Diadazzio looked absolutely livid. His mouth
worked, but no words came out. Before he could speak,
the man standing next to him dropped a heavy hand on his
shoulder.

"Simmer down, Albert," he said quietly. He turned to
Tess. "You're the lady with the talk show, aren't you?"
he asked, and the sympathy in his brown eyes told Tess he
not only had placed her but had connected her with Zach.

He was, as she had noted before, a large man, almost

clumsy looking, with arms a bit too long and hands that, though oversized, gave a curious sense of gentleness. He smiled—an immensely kind smile—and Tess, overcome by an impression of bigness and solidness, could only nod.

"Al, I think you might want to do what Mrs. Bondurant is asking," he said. Tess wondered who he was and what control he had over the man who looked dwarfed beside him. He was not a handsome man; in fact, his nose was slightly crooked, but he was handsomely dressed in a summer suit tailored perfectly to his imperfect build.

She spoke meekly now, with a look of gratitude toward him before directing herself with earnest apology to Dr. Diadazzio.

"Please, Doctor, forgive me for saying the things I did just now. I had no right. But the fact is, there *are* things we avoid talking about when we talk about children—things that you could address, and because of your considerable following you'd carry a great deal of weight."

"Her son was involved in an accident over the weekend," the unknown man beside him put in once again. "A group of children playing with a gun. Another child was killed."

"Oh, dear." Dr. Diadazzio gave a grave little bow toward Tess, and if there was in his manner none of the ebullience of his stage performance, she could nonetheless detect a genuine concern. "I am sorry. And yes, there are topics that are too often avoided because they cause discomfort, but—" He looked almost beseechingly at his companion. "Forrest, you know I couldn't possibly—not television—"

"Let's talk about it over lunch," said Forrest, who was, Tess decided, perhaps his manager. "Why don't you meet us out at the Holiday Inn, Mrs. Bondurant? I'll work on him on the way. Oh, and this would definitely be for your show, not an on-the-spot interview. What day?"

"Tomorrow?" Tess felt confident she could juggle her schedule for any day this week.

"How about Thursday? He's got a flight out that afternoon and can leave town ahead of the lynch mob, so to speak.''

"That's fine."

"We'll see you shortly, then."

The two men turned away, accompanied by the program lady, who had been making impatient signals.

"I'll bet you don't see them," said Katie under her breath. The camera was on her shoulder. Tess wondered if she had been filming any of this.

"Because these speakers are always expected to lunch with the officers of the group that's sponsoring them?" Tess asked, picking up her train of thought. "You may be right." Her spirits, which had risen with the easy optimism of the man called Forrest, slumped. "Oh, well, drop me there, and you can head on back. If they don't show—or even if they do—I'll call a cab."

Chapter Five

KATIE PROVED TO BE HALF RIGHT IN HER PREDICTIONS. Dr. Albert Diadazzio did not show up. As Tess was sitting alone at their appointed meeting place, however, toying with the cup of coffee she'd ordered in lieu of a drink, a broad set of shoulders appeared in the entrance to the dining room, and the man named Forrest made his way toward her.

"Slight change of plans." He smiled as he eased into the chair across from her. "My brother got snagged for lunch with the ladies who brought him here. Felt he couldn't in all conscience wiggle out of it."

"Brother?" said Tess. "Oh." She noticed now that he had the same curling brown hair as the man who had paced the lecture stage. He grinned, and the effect was even nicer than his smile, lightening his not-handsome face and suggesting a personality as strongly defined as his body was.

"Forrest Diadazzio," he said, engulfing her hand in the large paw he reached across the table. "Albert deals in toilet training, and I deal in impacted wisdom teeth. I'm an oral surgeon. We cover the market top to bottom, you might say.

"Couldn't you do with something stronger than coffee after what you must've been through the past few days? I know I could, and I've only sat through Albert's lecture."

Tess looked rather vacantly down at the cup of cold coffee.

"I suppose I could. I don't really know why I ordered this. It just seemed—" She shrugged. "About your brother—"

"He really did have the other engagement, and I didn't know it. I don't make a habit of asking married ladies to have lunch with me. Not even attractive ones." He smiled and looked at her fingers with interest. "But you don't wear rings."

Removing her hands from the table, Tess hid them in her lap and then felt foolish.

"I'm divorced," she said in a low voice. "I meant, will your brother be on my show?"

"I drove him to his appointment so we could talk about it. Yes, he will. However—" He seemed to hesitate, to measure her. "You must give him a list of the questions you intend to ask and stick to it religiously. Albert insists."

"But why?" It was the same stipulation he'd made for the other interview he'd given, she recalled. "I don't work that way. It would sound so stilted. And I certainly don't make it a habit of asking unpleasant questions or putting my guests on the spot in any way!"

"I know." He looked slightly amused. "My nurse watches part of your show on her coffee break on mornings we don't do surgery. I've seen it a few times. That's how I recognized you."

Tess felt embarrassed. Here was a man who had studied her image, formed whatever kind of opinions about her, and that created a sense of intimacy that somehow disturbed her even though she knew very well the intimacy did not exist.

"My brother's very shy," the man across from her said. "Extremely shy. He's only been on television once before, and he found it devastating."

"But he must give lectures like the one today frequently enough—and the people in the audience don't turn in their questions in writing."

For a moment, Forrest Diadazzio, with his slightly crooked nose and friendly brown eyes, looked as though he might reveal something. Then a slight frown wrinkled his forehead. He looked vaguely out across the dining room.

"I expect he gets the same questions in every audience. He could probably answer them in his sleep. Anyway, those are his terms. Take them or leave them. Oh, yes. And no questions about if he's got a wife and kids."

Tess sighed. "I'll take them. I'll drop the questions off to him tomorrow if you'll tell me where he's staying."

"I'll pick them up."

"All right. And he'll need to be at the station no later than ten on Thursday morning. Now," she added quickly as from the corner of her eye she saw a waiter approaching to take their order, "I think I'd better be on my way and not stay for lunch. I've got work to catch up on." *And I want to be home before Zach is*, she thought. She stood up and put out her hand in a gesture of departure. "I really am extremely grateful for your help in arranging this."

He rose, apparently willing enough to let her leave, yet as his hand once again folded over hers, Tess felt some invisible force bidding her to stay. Had her first impression of him been one of clumsiness? It had been wrong, for she felt the alert and deft sensitivity in each finger touching her.

Then she became aware of the two of them standing there without speaking even though it could only have been for the briefest of seconds.

"Teresa." A cold voice spoke from beyond the table, intruding.

Tess turned, and her heart sank in a swamp of discomfited guilt—guilt that she knew she didn't deserve but toward which that single word and tone of voice had pushed her. She was looking into the always-superior eyes and round, beige framed glasses of the woman who once had been her mother-in-law.

"Lucille," she said, and sat down again in her dismay. From the look of contempt being turned on her, she knew Lucille had judged and damned what, after all, had been just a parting handshake. *And here I'd assumed nothing I did could make me sink any lower in her opinion*, Tess thought with bleak amusement.

"Do you know Mr.—Dr. Diadazzio?" she asked, recovering. "He's helping me line up a guest for my show."

"I see," said Lucille, her cupid-bow lips scarcely moving in a face surrounded by carefully tended ash-blonde hair. She flicked a look of disgust at Forrest and then back at Tess. "I must say I'm surprised to see you out today. You're certainly none the worse for what happened to Zachary, are you?"

Without waiting for Tess's answer, she walked with clipped steps toward a table and exchanged a well-bred embrace with a woman waiting there, some old friend who was passing through and had stopped here near the Interstate, no doubt.

"Who was that?" asked Forrest, easing back into his chair.

"Zach's grandmother," Tess said in a tight voice.

"They make pretty good martinis here. I think we'd better try a couple." He nodded to a waiter who had been standing, none too graciously, beside the table.

But Tess was hurt by the accusation she'd seen in Lucille's eyes. The woman clearly thought this was some romantic rendezvous and that Tess was flitting gaily about while Zach suffered alone.

"Thank you, but no," she said. She went out to the lobby and called a cab.

Back in the studio parking lot, she made an abrupt decision. Getting into her car, she headed for home. If Earle was considering firing her, maintaining a spotless record for one afternoon would hardly dissuade him, she reasoned. All in all, she'd have done better staying at home today.

Attempting to keep her spirits up, she thought of all the other jobs the years with Bill had equipped her for if Channel 31 gave her the boot. She could sell shoes, she could clerk in a bakery, she could— But tears squeezed out. She loved what she was doing now. And she didn't have academic credentials for it, as did Heather. She didn't think her chances were good of being hired by another station.

Tess blew her nose vigorously, navigating with one hand. She couldn't afford to let herself go like this.

"Home so soon?" asked Whitmore, who watched over the house and Zach five days a week, as Tess came in. The older woman patted the mug of coffee sitting beside her. "Want some?"

Tess threw herself into a chair. "Yes, please. A man I'd never met before tried to help me through the rough spots by offering to buy me a martini. Right now I wish I'd taken him up on it."

Whitmore snorted.

"If he offered you a martini, *that* wasn't what he was trying."

The first grin in hours touched Tess's lips.

"Lucille didn't think so either when she saw us."

"That overage clotheshorse!" Whitmore set the coffee down so hard it spilled. "That's why she called to ask if you were home yet. I might have known it wouldn't be to offer help."

Tess sighed, knowing Whitmore had switched sides and was firmly in her camp now regarding a man's intentions in buying her drinks.

"Another misstep in the life and times of Tess Bondurant," she said with false cheer. "How's Zach?"

Whitmore shook her iron-gray head.

"Just picked at his breakfast, poor little guy." She paused. "The Rowe funeral's not going to be till Saturday," she said. "One set of the grandparents was out of the country, or something like that. Thought you should know."

Tess nodded. Here was something else about which to worry. Should she go to the funeral, or would her very presence there seem an insult? When Whitmore was gone, she watched the hands of the kitchen clock dig in and refuse to move.

She should get up—do laundry—but when she made the effort, hunting for something to distract herself, she found that Whitmore had beaten her to the chore. At last, she went into the living room and stood at the window. Zach's progress home from school, when he came into view, was very like the day before.

"Katie asked about you," she said, smoothing back his hair when they were in the house. "She says there's a movie she and Leroy want to take you to see."

Silence met her efforts.

"How was school?"

"Okay."

Should she ask how the kids were treating him? Who his true friends were these days? It was delicate territory.

"I got the parcheesi board out," she said instead. "Let's have a game."

Zach looked at her, and his eyes were tired, with dark shadows.

"I don't feel like parcheesi. Can I go to my room?"

Feeling defeated, and frightened by that defeat, Tess watched him move away from her. Before he disappeared, she tried again.

"I'm afraid I forgot to get groceries. What do you say we have supper at the pancake house?"

It was his favorite outing, morning or night. He never refused.

"No, thanks. I'm not hungry," he said.

A few seconds later, Tess heard him close his bedroom door.

Like a door between us, like a door between him and the rest of his life, she thought in anguish. *How am I ever going to help him?*

Chapter Six

AS SHE WALKED OUT TO HER CAR IN THE LIFTING DARK-
ness the following morning, Tess's eyes froze on dim
shapes on the garage door. Letters. Spray-painted. Crude.
A single word:

KILLER

Limbs shaking with rage, she marched swiftly to the
garage and flung up the heavy door. Then she backtracked
to the house and stuck her head inside.

"Whitmore. Leave the garage door up," she ordered
shortly.

If the lawn mower, Zach's new ten-speed, anything
else, was stolen, she did not care.

"Damn!" she said, striking the steering wheel with
clenched fists and tasting new and unfamiliar bitterness.
"Damn!"

After all the good times she and Zach had had in that
neighborhood, she thought. After being good neighbors—
taking soup or a casserole in when someone was sick,
shoveling snow for the elderly Davisons. Twenty minutes
later, when she pulled to a stop in front of the studio, Tess
could remember no details of the morning's drive.

That word on the garage had been scrawled by an adult,
she felt certain. It hadn't been there when Whitmore arrived or she would have seen it, and the chances of a child

41

being up by the time Tess left for work were nonexistent. But who would have done such a thing, she asked herself? And was it a preview of what was to come?

Yesterday Tess had pulled out a small pet-shop feature that she and Katie had put together recently. She would do that on her usual eight o'clock slot. No more giving people in the station a chance to say she wasn't carrying her part of the load. No more all-night bakeries.

"Hi, Tess. How're things at home?" asked P. T. Porter, the station's overworked but always smiling production assistant, as Tess came in.

"They're getting better." Tess knew her tone must sound strangely grim. She could hardly unload about the graffiti to anyone who'd listen, though, could she?

"I dropped some things off on your desk," said P. T. "Your sked for 'Tess and Guests' still firm for the rest of the week?"

Tess shuffled through the fresh pile of papers and envelopes P. T. had left her, most of them press releases, a few letters from viewers.

"Oh, great. Another hot speaker the Home and Hearth League wants me to make time for, I see."

P. T. wrinkled her nose. "That's that nutty group you had on about three months ago, isn't it? The one that wants to outlaw day-care centers?"

"*And* family planning clinics *and* women with minor children working except in a family business *and* who knows what else." Tess tossed down a press release. *I seem to have proved the dangers of the working part they love to talk about*, she thought with fleeting uneasiness. "We've given them a forum for their views. I don't know what more they want. They can't seem to understand we've got a policy about how often any one group's on. They've been inundating me and the news desk both with announcements of their pseudospeakers."

Sighing slightly, Tess slipped her coat off and dropped it across her desk.

"Oh, well, part of the job, I guess. No, to answer your

question about my sked. Dr. Diadazzio, a child psychiatrist, will be on tomorrow.''

Yesterday, at home, Tess had called the chairman of this year's summer arts festival. The woman had been so eager to have the publicity for her group that an appearance on Tess's show would generate that she had been more than willing when Tess asked her to postpone until the following week.

Tess sat down to read through the rest of her mail. Perhaps once a week the practice yielded an idea for something she could use.

Today there was a note on a cat show at a shopping mall. If she did a segment on that, it would mean she'd used two animal stories in less than a week, but they were proven favorites. Perhaps she could try an unusual angle: the child who was putting a beloved pet on display on the one hand and a professional cat breeder on the other.

One thing about it, she noted uneasily, Josh didn't seem about to flood her with work this week. There usually was a daily message in her typewriter—things she must cover or things she might. Today there was none. She frowned.

In front of her, the phone shrilled. With a leap of fear, she put out her hand. This couldn't be about Zach; he was barely out of bed by this time, she reassured herself. It was Bill's voice, angry, that came to her across the wire.

''Damn it, Tess, it's bad enough that you go off and leave Zach alone in the middle of this,'' he began without preliminaries. ''But do you also have to flit around having lunch and making ga-ga eyes with some man where everyone can see?''

Tess tried to control the slow rage spreading inside her. First that word sprayed on the garage and now this. What a start to her day.

''I was hardly making ga-ga eyes, as you put it,'' she said carefully. ''It was a business appointment.''

''That's not how my mother saw it.''

''And how does she see you and Caroline? As a pair of utter innocents, no doubt. If Lucille's so concerned about

43

Zach, she might try seeing him more than twice a year—''
Tess stopped and brushed a hand across her forehead.
''I'm sorry, Bill. Can we talk some other time? I'm fright-
fully busy—''

''And out of sorts, it appears.'' He sounded wounded
now, and Tess felt embarrassed over the things she'd said.

''Yes, I am, as a matter of fact. When I came out to get
in the car this morning, someone had painted a—something
about Zach on our garage door.''

''About what you could expect in that working-class
neighborhood,'' he said with a knowing air.

''Three teachers and a social worker two doors up hardly
qualifies it as working class!'' She slammed down the
phone. ''And by the way, your support check's late—
again,'' she added under her breath. Why couldn't Bill
ever unbend? He'd never called her at work before, and it
upset her.

''Touchy, Tess?''

Earle stood at the desk behind her, watching her. His
blond-white eyebrows arched mildly.

Tess started to deny it, then thought better.

''I'm afraid dealing with an ex-spouse is one of those
things I find difficult.''

''I can appreciate that. I have one myself.'' He gave a
wry grimace.

Tess looked at him uncertainly. It was the first time she
had heard that fact about Earle, the only thing she knew
about him apart from life at the station, really.

He moved on, but the episode left a knot in her stomach. Was he watching her, monitoring her emotions, judging? Absently, she picked up a ceramic mug, starting for
the electric coffee urn that sat on the far side of the corral.
The pudgy reporter who sat in front of her stuck his mug
out.

''Since you're going, how about bringing me one? Extra
sugar.''

Tess took his mug without comment, thinking it was
miraculous how he only needed coffee when she was

going. If the lazy lug had to go himself, he'd probably get a hernia. He never expected the same treatment from the men who passed his desk, but it was a minor irritant, and Tess was generally too busy to make a scene.

"Hey, shouldn't you be downstairs?" asked Katie, joining her at the coffee urn.

In surprise, Tess glanced at the large clock on the wall above them.

"Oh, rats!" she said. It already was time for the meeting preceding the eight o'clock news. Even the clock appeared to be her enemy this morning. She felt the need to pick on someone in return. With a small grin of mischief, she set down the mug belonging to the pudgy reporter. She wondered how many days would pass before he realized she'd quit delivering coffee.

"Glad you could join us," said Josh in a snide tone as she slid into place on the news set, the last to arrive. "You look as though you had one hell of a night."

It was meant to unnerve her, she knew, this implication she didn't look polished enough to go "on camera." Tess looked at him levelly.

"And I'd say you looked like a man worn out by his own performance."

He gave her a glacial glare.

You may regret that, Tess, she told herself. But it had been worth it. She had tried her best to get along with Josh. If he was set on being unpleasant—was even willing to cut her throat for his girl friend's sake—then what was the point in playing Little Miss Nice? Perhaps she had already let herself be shoved into that role by too many people.

The red eye of a camera blinked to life. Matt Saxton began to recap the news in a mellow bass voice. Tess and her pet-shop feature came after the news of a gas-line rupture and before the 31-Weather. Twenty-eight minutes later, the camera blinked off.

By the time she welcomed her own guest, Tess felt tense. *Don't let there be any calls like yesterday*, she prayed as they walked downstairs. Today's program was about a cookbook by a local men's group—surely not controversial. Still, as the end of the program arrived and the phone lines were thrown open, she had the sensation of her shoulders hunching upward as though to protect herself.

Then Jack was giving her the finish sign.

"A good one, Tessie."

She let her eyes flutter closed for a second in unspoken relief.

When Tess stepped outside the studio, Agnes, the receptionist, was waiting. An ancient creature with intensely red hair, she slipped her wrinkled hand through Tess's arm and patted it reassuringly.

"I've only had three calls complaining about you this morning," she whispered. "And I won't mention any of them to the folks upstairs."

Tess was startled and touched by this offering from a woman she knew more as a voice on the phone than someone visited with in person. But then Agnes had always been a good egg, putting Zach through to her promptly if he sounded truly worried, chiding him gently if he called about some trifle. The other jobs Tess had held made her appreciate Agnes as a rarity. Never once had the receptionist ever complained about the extra chores created by mothers whose children called them at work.

"Thank you, Agnes. That means a lot," Tess said.

Wagging her red head, Agnes started back to guard her lobby. She'd gone only a few steps when she looked back in afterthought.

"Of course I don't know how many of the calls I've put through to the bigwigs might have been the same thing," she added.

"I'm sure I'll find out," Tess said grimly.

But she heard nothing, and that in itself made her uneasy. It was hard to concentrate on the questions she was preparing for Albert Diadazzio. At half past two, she put them aside in an envelope marked with his name and headed for home.

As she started her car, the engine made a squealing sound. She turned it off, too despondent even for cursing; knowing what she would find, she got out and raised the hood.

"Troubles?" asked a voice behind her.

She turned to see Forrest Diadazzio leaning over the door of a cinnamon-colored car.

"Oh, it's my fan belt," she said through set teeth. "I knew it was coming loose, but I've put off getting it fixed. Now it's too late, by the look of things."

She shrugged, making light of the problem even though she was beginning to wonder in desperation how many she'd be called upon to face today. "I didn't expect you by until much later. I thought you'd probably stop by after office hours. There's an envelope with your brother's name on it at the reception desk. Please tell him I promise not to deviate from the questions."

He smiled, not an outgoing man but one who intrigued her by his very quietness.

"We seem to be having similar days," he said, nodding toward her car. "I didn't schedule office hours this week since I knew Albert would be here, but then I got called in this morning for emergency surgery. Traffic accident. A man got his jaw broken in three places and lost most of his teeth. I just finished up. Figured I might as well stop by here while I was out and about."

Tess noticed now the shadow of beard on his face. It made him look rough-hewn, especially with that slightly crooked nose and large physique. He glanced at the raised hood of her car.

"The fan belt, huh? I'm afraid I'm not even sure which part that is. Why don't you let me drive you home? I expect you're anxious to be there when your little boy gets home from school."

Tess knew she ought to refuse; only he was right about Zach. If she called a cab, there was no telling how long she'd wait, and the gas-station road service would take even longer.

47

"It's a terrible imposition—" she said lamely.

"Nonsense!" He gestured to the car behind him. "Just let me go inside and get that envelope."

Tess slammed the hood of her own car and slid into his with a feeling of relief. Arrangements with the service station could wait until later. Just now she was grateful that for the moment she didn't have to cope.

The car she was sitting in was comfortable but not extravagant. She ran her finger tips over the soft velour seats. Forrest Diadazzio's suit jacket was thrown carelessly in the back. He must be exhausted, she thought, yet he had offered to make this detour.

"Actually, there is a woman who's there when Zach gets home. A neighbor who comes in and watches things for me while I'm at work," she said with some guilt when he had returned. "But I am especially anxious to be there—well, just now. I really do thank you."

"Sure thing." He inclined his head. "Do you have others besides him—Zach?"

"No." Tess looked out the window. "It's just the two of us."

"Nice place," he said when they turned into the entrance to the cul-de-sac. "Quiet."

"Nice place for kids to play." Tess gave a faded smile. "Or so I thought."

"You don't blame yourself for what happened, do you?" he asked.

They had reached her house. Tess shook her head.

"Not really. I try to tell myself no one's to blame. But it's hard." Her voice grew more forceful as she remembered the morning's graffiti. "It's awfully hard."

"I'll bet it is." There was something in the softness of his words that made her think he understood. All at once, as he struggled to hold it back, he yawned.

Tess laughed and opened the car door. "I'm afraid you're going to fall asleep driving out of here. Whitmore— the woman who helps me—always has a pot of coffee ready by this time. Wouldn't you like some?"

"I guess I'd better," he said ruefully. "Say, just how early do you go in if this is your quitting time?"

She grinned at him. "You don't want to know."

Then she felt almost disgusted with herself that she could be so lighthearted with a man at a time like this.

A woman with a toddler following her came out to check the mail on the porch next door just then. Tess lifted a hand in a subdued wave.

"Hi, Laurel."

The woman looked at her, through her, turned, and went back in. Tess felt a lump rise in her throat. Was Laurel going to shut them out because of the accident? Or could the frosty treatment, she suddenly wondered, have something to do with the fact she was being brought home by an unknown man?

She shook the thought off angrily. A snub was a snub, and the cause didn't matter. Whitmore made welcoming noises, brought coffee, and left for the day.

"I'd better not—I might never get up," said Forrest when she offered a chair. He leaned against a bookcase and drank his coffee in quick sips as though in need of it. "Anyway, I don't want to make you run late for any plans you've got with your son."

"Plans!" Tess made a despairing gesture. "I can't even get him to talk. I'm hoping your brother will be kind enough to counsel me on my own for just a minute or two tomorrow. I'm getting close to my wit's end."

He put his empty cup on a coaster on a nearby table.

"Don't worry, Albert barks a lot more than he bites. He's actually a pretty great guy. Mind you, I would never have thought it back in the days when I was stuck with a little brother who couldn't keep up with me."

Tess smiled at the image conjured up and put her cup down next to his. "You mean little-younger or little-little?"

He chuckled as though he liked the question.

"Both senses, I guess. He's two years younger than me."

That made Forrest Diadazzio forty, Tess thought, recalling the résumé on his brother she'd reviewed that afternoon. And then the doorbell rang, and she flinched, surprised to find herself so jumpy.

"Now who can that—" She opened the door and swallowed the last word. "Bill!"

If she had not expected to see him, he clearly had not expected to find another man in the room. The expression that crossed his face was one of indignation. Tess could almost read what was in his mind as he stared at Forrest, and she was amused. In his shirt-sleeves, with his shadow of beard, Forrest looked more like an itinerant lumberjack than an oral surgeon. Yet she felt awkward, too, as though she had done something wrong.

"Well, thanks for the coffee, Mrs. Bondurant. I'd better be going," said Forrest. "Want me to have someone stop by and take care of your car?"

She shook her head, struck by the grace with which he handled the situation.

"I'm afraid I brought my keys home with me. I'll have somebody see to it tomorrow."

She held the door as he stepped past Bill with a pleasant nod. Mrs. Bondurant, she thought. He had said that deliberately. It had been an attempt to spare her any discomfort.

Bill gave her a long and nettling look from behind long lashes as she closed the door.

"Well, I must say, Tess, I'm surprised to find your taste in boy friends runs toward orangutans."

She flushed, hoping Forrest Diadazzio had not heard.

"Damn it, Bill, did you have to—"

"It was just a joke." He held up his hands.

Wouldn't you know he'd see her with the same man Lucille had, Tess thought crossly. But then what business was it of theirs, even if she *had* been seeing Forrest under the most innocent circumstances?

"He's just someone who happened to give me a ride home," she said mildly, refusing to rise to the argument he was trying to start. "The fan belt gave out on my car. I've been putting off getting it fixed until my bank account looked better."

Bill looked immediately huffy at the perceived insinuation.

"I'll write you a check when I get home. I don't have my checkbook."

It was a line Tess had heard before. Bill knew she'd never resort to anything unpleasant if the check never came.

"What did you stop by about? Is something the matter?" she asked now. It was unusual for Bill to take time off work.

He gave an attractive shrug. "I just thought I should check and see if you needed anything. You didn't sound like yourself on the phone this morning."

Tess turned to the bookcase where Forrest had stood and pushed the spine of a book into line with her finger.

"I'm not myself. I'm scared about Zach. The other kids appear to have deserted him, at least for the time being, which is natural, I suppose, but he's—so lost—so—I don't know." In silent misery, she shook her head.

"I don't like this business about the graffiti, Tess."

She started to reply, but then the door opened, and Zach came in.

"Dad!" His small face, which had grown pale in the last two days, seemed to brighten.

"Hello, Zachary. How are you doing, Tiger?" Bill wooled Zach's hair, then bent to produce a sack Tess hadn't noticed from beneath his arm. "Thought you might like a new catcher's mitt, old buddy. Help cheer you up."

Zach's eyes widened with a hopefulness that tugged at Tess's heart.

"Oh, *boy*! Can we go try it out?"

"Not today, son. I'm busy." Bill straightened. "I just stopped by to see your mom about a couple of things."

Tess held out a hand, inviting Zach for a hug, but he ignored her. In silence, he turned and walked, more slowly now, toward his room.

"Bill, if you could spend just a few minutes with him—make him feel there's someone else willing to claim him—"

"I can't, Tess. Not today."

"What about letting him spend the weekend with you?"

Bill looked embarrassed for once.

"I promised Caroline I'd take her somewhere Saturday. She's been counting on it for weeks. Look, Tess, I'm sorry. I'll do something with him soon. I promise. But we've got to talk about this—this—"

He waved his hand.

"I don't think it's wise of you to go on living in this neighborhood. I think you should move."

Tess folded her arms, not wanting to hear someone else voice the thoughts she herself was entertaining.

"You mean uproot Zach? Make him feel it's his fault that we can't stay here? I don't think that's wise."

Bill brushed the words aside as though they were frivolous.

"What's the alternative? Stay here and let them smear the whole house with graffiti?"

She swallowed. "Maybe that won't happen again."

"And what about the other kids turning on him? You admitted yourself not two minutes ago that was happening. By God, what right do those other brats have to snub him, anyway? They're the ones who got him into this. Zach's a cut above them to start with. He's bright. He should be in a neighborhood where he can make friends with kids from better backgrounds. He doesn't belong here."

His superior tone was making Tess feel rebellious now. She sat down, head shaking in disbelief. Bill made it sound as though she and Zach were living in some ghetto. He liked to orchestrate things, but he had no concept of practicalities.

"Do you have the slightest idea what the mere difference in the interest rate on a mortgage would be?" she asked.

"I've already talked to my mother. She's willing to make you a loan."

Overcome by the strain of things, Tess began to laugh erratically.

"A loan! That's just dandy. Did you know I could lose my job at the station because of this? What do you expect me to do then, Bill? Sell pencils on the corner?"

"I can see you don't want to discuss it," he said stiffly. "I'll call tomorrow when you've had a chance to think."

She did not see him to the door, but leaned back, eyes closed, feeling drained. Zach's voice, speaking at her elbow, startled her.

"Mom?"

She looked quickly up to see him watching her, wide-eyed. At least his eyes were alert, she thought, but his face was miserable.

"Are we going to have to move? Does everyone hate us that much?"

Tess flung her arms around him.

"I don't know, Zach. I just don't know."

He clung to her, and she held him tightly.

"Are you really going to lose your job?" he asked in muffled tones.

"Oh, Zach—I don't think so. I was—I was just angry with your father and feeling lonesome and mixed up—maybe sort of like you're feeling now."

He was silent for the longest moment. Then, for the first time since he'd come in with blood dripping from his hands, Zach started to sob.

Tess felt panic fill her, felt it slowly receding as her arms enfolded him. It was good this dam breaking. If Zach could cry—if he could *feel*—he surely would mend.

Nonetheless, it hurt to see his agony.

"You are lonesome, aren't you? It's crummy, huh?" She tried to coax him into sharing feelings.

"I hate it! I wish it had been me instead of Andy!" He shouted the words.

Tess winced. This raw emotion was much more than she'd bargained for.

Had she been wrong to stir it up? She didn't know now. She wondered. In spite of the ugliness of this moment, she would simply have to hope it was for the good.

Chapter Seven

By TEN-FIFTEEN THE FOLLOWING MORNING TESS WAS
frantic. Albert Diadazzio had not arrived and had not called.

"He's not going to show," she said, pacing at the edge
of her set as Katie looked on. "Good God, what will I do?"

"What you've always said you'd do if something like
this happened," Katie said. "Interview me and tell everyone how they get those marvelous news clips on their
screens."

"You have an assignment to get to."

"I'll shove it off on someone else."

"By the way, have I asked you to thank Leroy for
fixing my fan belt and leaving the car at my doorstep?"

"Three times, last count. Handy being wed to a cop
who knows how to hotwire, huh?"

Just then, the studio door opened, and P. T. looked
wildly in.

"He's here," she announced.

Albert Diadazzio, followed by Forrest, was at her heels.

"My cheering section," the child-care expert said wanly.
"I came late so I wouldn't have time enough to lose my
nerve. I hope you don't mind."

Katie, sticking a thumb up in encouragement, left. P. T.
was already hustling Forrest to a spot on the sidelines and
giving him orders. Tess led Albert to the yellow couch
with its aura of homeyness, and Jack came forward with
his card to check the light.

"Let's put these on the table," said Tess, taking the two books on child care that her guest had authored and that he was juggling in one hand as if he had no idea what to do with them.

"What?" he asked distractedly. "Oh, yes."

Good heavens, what if the man fell apart completely, Tess thought? As lights went on, she began to speak quickly, telling him what to expect, coaching him to look at the camera.

"I may not ask my questions in the exact same order they were on my list," she said. "But it will be pretty close, and I won't throw you anything new. I promise."

Jack was holding up his fingers now, counting down the seconds. A camera began to move in. Dr. Albert Diadazzio smiled at her like a cherub.

"Please don't worry, but I've decided to pick a topic of my own choosing instead of your questions," he said as Jack's last finger went down and the program aired.

For a split second, Tess was too stunned to force her tongue to release itself. The theme music was already rolling, as it always did on Tuesday and Thursday, allowing no break before they started. With the feeling of one who'd been booted off a trapeze and had no certainty of a net below, she began to talk.

"Good Thursday morning. I'm Tess Bondurant, and my guest today is Dr. Albert Diadazzio, the noted child psychiatrist. Many of you have read his very helpful books—" she knew the camera was picking them up right now— "and perhaps some of you were fortunate enough to hear him speak here Tuesday on the common problems we all face in child rearing.

"Today, however, we're going to be talking about something different. I think." She gave a quick grin. "To tell the truth, Dr. Diadazzio informed me just as we went on the air that he had his own ideas about what we should discuss this morning, so I think I'll just sit back and let him tell all of us."

The man beside her was peering rather too intently into

the camera. Already his forehead was starting to glimmer with sweat. But something of the zeal that had propelled him in his speech two days before was also in evidence. He nodded gravely, cleared his throat, and began.

"I feel I must talk to you today about the unhappy things which a child psychiatrist sees—not the everyday things which one parent can discuss easily with another but the special concerns of the child who knows he is dying, of the retarded child, of the child who has been somehow involved in a terrible accident and holds himself guilty."

He turned to Tess and touched her hand.

"Mrs. Bondurant—Tess—I commend your courage in asking me to come and speak about these things. I know this is a painful time in your personal life—your son and other children playing with a gun, a little boy dead."

Inwardly, Tess gasped. Then, slowly, a wonderful feeling of relief spread over her. There. It was out in the open now, and she was glad.

"Because we don't talk about such things as we do sibling rivalry, for example," Albert was saying, "we too often don't realize what a friend, or even a relative, may be suffering. And we give the parents and child involved a sense of isolation.

"But you are not isolated. Do you know, for example, how many children have been killed playing with guns in your state of Ohio in the past five years?" He pulled a slip of paper from his pocket. "Your local police department was kind enough to furnish me with some figures."

He was speaking quietly but with fervor. After the figures, he went on to describe the confusion of real-versus-not-real that children faced in a society where they were allowed to play with toy machine guns, where video games in which things were eaten or blown up or otherwise destroyed had become the rage, where televised fiction showed people dying but it was pretend.

"Parents need to talk to their children about these things," he said. "They need to talk about values not only to their children but to each other. And let me add here that I don't

57

necessarily mean"—he stopped, in sudden and awkward contrast to his flowing style, then finished abruptly—"religious values. Now let's discuss children with handicaps, mental and physical. . . ."

Tess was hard pressed to keep the tears from her eyes, he spoke with such loving concern. She could not imagine why he had been so reticent to be on her program. He had so much to say and so little time in which to say it. Before Tess was willing for it to be time, he was concluding.

"As a society, we need to work very hard on having more compassion," he said.

Then the calls began.

The first was from a woman who was weeping softly.

"I want to thank you, doctor," she said. "And thank you, Tess. My son accidentally tipped his sister out of an infant seat on a counter when she was two months old, and she suffered brain damage. It's been four years now, and it's still—it's so hard for our family. This has helped."

The others were less touching, mere questions, for which Tess was grateful.

"Please—write a book on this," one caller urged.

Then they were off.

The instant she knew they were, Tess leaned across and kissed Albert on the cheek.

"You were magnificent," she said, choking over the words.

"You mean we're finished?" he said blankly. Sinking back, he looked at his surroundings as if for the first time. "Oh, G-G-God. I m——" An inarticulate sound, like an animal lowing, issued from him before he controlled his tongue again. "I made it!"

Forrest was striding forward. Extending both arms, he caught his brother's shoulder in a congratulatory clap.

"Well done, Al! I knew you could do it."

Albert smiled weakly. "You owe me a fifth of the best scotch I'm able to find."

The phone on one wall, which brought word from the

rest of the building, flashed its light silently. P. T., standing nearby, picked it up.

"It's Agnes," she said, covering the mouthpiece. "She says the switchboard's jammed—and all the calls so far have been raves!"

There was no need for quiet in the studio now. For the next hour, they were plugged into old sitcom reruns. Jack and the others crowded around, complimenting Tess and the doctor.

"Jesus," said one of the cameramen shaking his head. "My little nephew's spastic, and I guess I really never understood how hard that is on my sister-in-law, you know?"

As they started out into the hall, Albert spoke to Tess.

"How's your little boy doing?"

She drew a breath. "I don't know. It's sort of the way that woman who called in first explained it—he's behind a wall."

"He's got a good mother to see him through it. That helps."

She smiled, appreciating his reassurance.

"I wish I felt that I were helping."

"It takes time. Relatives can do a lot. Easing him into the world, doing things with him. Letting him know there are still people who think he's okay."

Matt Saxton came springing down the back stairs, a pleased expression on his face.

"That was great, Tess! If that doesn't get us some kind of award, I'll eat my hat. And some man just called. He didn't say what the problem was, but he said for the first time in months he and his wife didn't feel so alone."

He looked up as Earle came out of the first-floor corridor to the business offices just behind them.

"What do you say, Earle?" Matt pressed. "Wasn't it great? We haven't had this much viewer response over anything local in years!"

The station manager smiled, but the smile was wintry.

"It was interesting, and I expect we've won more viewers for a few days. But it may interest all of you to know—Egyptian Queen Figure Salon has just called canceling all their advertising time with us."

Chapter Eight

TESS STARED AT HIM, NOT BELIEVING WHAT SHE WAS hearing. The figure salon was one of the main advertisers on her show.

"But why?" she gasped. "Why if the response was good?"

"They said they couldn't chance seeming to support your personal campaign against guns and that they didn't care to be associated with a woman who perhaps hadn't given proper supervision as a mother."

"Proper sup—"

"As to response," Earle continued, "I took one call from a woman who said if she wanted to listen to tasteless, depressing trash, she could watch 'Donahue'."

"Not in our time slot she couldn't," muttered P. T., but Tess, although she heard, was not amused.

"What campaign against guns? I didn't say one thing against guns," Tess protested. Nor had Albert Diadazzio. In fact, he had taken great pains to avoid the issue, prefacing his comments on toys and games by saying he would not presume to comment on the practice of keeping weapons in the home for self-defense.

"A perceived reprimand is all the same as a spoken one to advertisers," Earle said mildly. "You took a rather interesting gamble, Tess, counteracting adverse publicity. But Egyptian Queen says they won't spend another penny with us till you're off the air."

The statement turned her entrails to ice. Earle turned and walked up the stairs, with Matt hurrying after him.

Off the air! But—

Tess felt someone slip a supporting hand beneath her elbow and looked up in a daze to find it was Forrest Diadazzio.

"You look like a lady who needs to be taken to lunch," he said with a smile.

"I feel like a lady who needs to put her head in the oven. That dumb set doesn't have one, unfortunately."

Everyone else seemed to have scurried off in different directions. She freed herself and ran a hand through her hair, seeking control.

"Thank you," she said. "About lunch, I mean. But I really don't think I'd better."

He drew his eyebrows together, and Tess noted that it made him look rather forbidding.

"Why?"

A laugh that was much too close to hysteria sprang free of her.

"Well," she said, gesturing helplessly, "for one thing, it appears I'm about to be fired. And what about Albert?"

"Albert's on his way to the airport. Prearranged plans."

"Oh."

Now it was her turn to frown at him, trying to make sense of his last statement, though the events of the last few minutes had left her too upset to make much headway. Forrest smiled slightly.

"Some nerve, huh, especially considering that guy who was at your place yesterday has the added advantage of not looking like an orangutan. But, after all, it never hurts to try."

Tess was more than ever provoked at Bill for making that remark. And Forrest Diadazzio's acceptance of his lack of physical beauty touched her. She tried to smile back but was afraid she failed.

"I haven't made the acquaintance of any orangutans

lately, so I couldn't comment on that,'' she said steadily. ''And that guy, unfortunately, is Zach's father.''

She stopped, surprised at herself. Whatever had prompted her to say ''unfortunately''? Nerves giving away, she supposed.

She hurried on quickly. ''I'd love to have lunch with you, Dr. Diadazzio—Forrest. But the way things are going just now, I'm afraid I might just end up crying all over the place.''

''That's okay as long as you don't order soup—might make it too salty.'' He offered his arm. ''Come on, there's a place down in Yellow Springs that might be serving outside on a nice day like today. I'll have you back here in an hour and fifteen minutes.''

In spite of his predictions, the weather was still too chill for outdoor dining. They were shown to seats beside a vacant fireplace inside a colorful little restaurant filled with mismatched wooden tables. The tables were unified by their identical Perrier bottles, each bearing a few sprigs of bright spring flowers. As Tess shifted slightly, the chair she was sitting in rocked, betraying one leg worn shorter than the other three, but she didn't mind. As she was persuaded by Forrest to try the day's special omelet, then heard him ordering Irish coffee for both of them, she found herself relaxing. She was surrounded by a sense, though it came fleetingly and then was gone again, of being cared for.

A silly thought, she told herself crossly. But there was something in Forrest Diadazzio that was quite unlike any other man she'd ever known.

''You know,'' she said. ''You're perfectly gallant, but I also think you must be warped. No one in their right mind would seek out the company of anyone as self-absorbed and weepy as I am these days.''

''No one's ever accused me of being in my right mind.'' He grinned slowly. ''Actually, I've just got this long-running fantasy of getting to rescue a damsel in distress.

Since you're on TV, I figure that puts you in the public domain. That makes it fair for me to practice on you."

Tess laughed. A look of satisfaction spread across his face.

"I knew I'd like the sound of it when you did that. Here we go."

Two mugs of Irish coffee were being set in front of them. With eyes half closed, Tess sipped the steaming liquid, letting the dab of whipped cream on top bump gently against her lip.

"Good?" asked Forrest as she opened her eyes and set the mug down.

"Yes. Very. Thank you." She studied him curiously: the strong lines of his face, the curly brown hair, the slight scar slanting down from one edge of his lower lip that she only now noticed. It was a face that had been through a lot, she thought. Yet from his quiet manner, his immaculate dress, even his profession, she found it hard to imagine his ever going in for anything like boxing or football. She found herself wondering many things about this man.

"Why didn't you tell me your brother was afraid of interviews because he stutters?" she asked. "Why didn't *he* tell me?"

He smiled, and she noticed again what a nice effect it had on his face.

"Embarrassment on Albert's part, I guess. He used to be much worse as a kid than he is now." His eyes flickered with a distant anger whose source eluded her. He looked away from her as though to control some change in moods.

"One of those childhood afflictions whose beginning confounds the experts," he said briefly. The harshness underlying his words was startling in someone she'd already come to think of as so easygoing. "Anyway," he added, more mildly now, "he's learned to control it over the years, and he's learned to avoid the situations where he thinks it might betray him. I'd never tell his secret. But then I was fairly sure he could handle your program, too."

His loyalty and the closeness so clearly existing between the two brothers warmed her. She wondered what he'd been thinking about to make him sound angry.

"Well, I think he's marvelous, and I don't give a damn if he did make a few people feel uncomfortable with what he said." She stabbed at the alfalfa sprouts, sprinkled with sunflower seeds, curling from her salad bowl. Of course she cared.

"They're not really serious about booting you out the door if they lose a few sponsors, are they?"

She shrugged. "I don't know. Probably. And I suppose in fairness it's just good business sense."

"Then what?"

"I don't know." She smiled at him ruefully. "I've got to have a job."

She saw the question in his eyes and was glad he did not voice it. What was wrong with her? She was revealing altogether too much of herself.

"I'll deal with that when I'm forced to," she said, more firmly than she'd intended. There was something about sitting here in the company of this large man that bolstered her courage. She eyed the arriving omelets, their just-set edges folded over sour cream, jalapeño peppers, onion and jack cheese, and felt an almost forgotten stirring of appetite.

"The thing I'm most concerned about right now is Zach," she said around her first mouthful. "I think your brother made me feel better about that—though goodness knows why, considering his advice was to turn to relatives for help in easing Zach into the world."

"Does that present a problem?"

"My parents are in Arizona. They were disappointed when I married Bill instead of finishing college and even more wearily disappointed when I called the marriage quits. It's not a situation where I'm comfortable asking for help. As a matter of fact, I haven't even worked up the courage to let them know what's happened here. And Bill's mother—" She broke off and laughed.

"Ah, yes. The lady who came upon us when we weren't

having lunch. Having someone that hostile around would sink any marriage, I'd think."

Tess avoided his eyes now, slightly embarrassed.

"As it happened, the marriage had a lot more going against it. I can't blame Lucille." She moved to a subject that she hoped was a safer corollary. "Is that why you warned me not to ask Albert about his marital status? Did he have a bad experience?"

He hesitated, and once again Tess saw something unspoken hovering in his eyes. Something unpleasant.

"No. Albert's never been married. Neither of us has." His tone grew lighter now. "We're both a couple of arrested adolescents, I guess, not ready to grow up quite yet. Albert's afraid that if people find out he doesn't have kids of his own, they'll be properly indignant wondering how he dares to tell everyone else how they should raise theirs."

"A question which could be voiced about every child-care expert around, I dare say, since they're all male and busy seeing patients and writing books."

He nodded soberly. "Want more coffee, Irish or plain?"

"No, thanks."

He rose and held her chair, and as her arm brushed his, Tess felt them both hesitate, prolonging the contact. Just as her appetite had stirred, some other sensation trembled inside her.

How could she, she asked in mild alarm? How could she respond to a man—any man—when all her thoughts just now should be for Zach?

"Thank you," she murmured again. She walked quickly ahead, taking care their bodies did not touch.

An hour and a half had elapsed by the time they drove the eight miles back to Springfield. As she walked into the station, Tess felt the new strength the respite had spawned in her slipping away.

The moment she reached her desk, Josh appeared out of nowhere.

"Nice you decided that you could spare a few hours with us," he said with dripping nastiness.

Tess gave him a hard look. "I was at lunch, as half the people up here must be, I see. Any objections?"

Josh removed the curving pipe from his mouth and gestured with it.

"Earle wants to see you."

Her stomach clutched together so tightly Tess was sure the two sides met.

Earle sat behind his desk with his feet up, light-blue polo shirt and darker blue pants complementing his eyes. He did not right himself as Tess came in.

"Well," he said when the silence had battered her nerves to the breaking point. "Josh and I have been talking. We think it will be best if Heather takes over your morning feature at least for a few weeks."

What did he expect? Agreement? Argument?

Tess drew a breath.

"I see."

"I'll want to see a list of the guests you've got lined up for next week, too," he said. "We want to make sure they're interesting, but we want to make damn sure they're not controversial. Two ladies from that damned Home and Hearth League have already been up to see me demanding equal time for what was said today."

"Good God, what did they disagree with? Do they think kids should be encouraged to run around hacking and shooting or that people with handicapped children should hide them in barrels or—"

"They seem to object to you primarily. They felt you were using the public air waves to justify working mothers, and they felt much of what your guest said was antifamily."

Tess shook her head, unable to believe what she was hearing. This was just an excuse. Earle was trying to make it so tough on her she'd quit voluntarily. Or was that merely wishful thinking?

"Well, you máy not like next Wednesday," she said. "And neither may they. A woman whose children were kidnaped by her ex is coming to talk about it. No doubt the ladies from Home and Hearth would say she wouldn't have any problem at all if she'd stayed married. I'm afraid we can't have people doing recipes from their cookbooks every day, Earle, and what's more, women today—most women—aren't bimbos enough to want it."

He stared in her general direction.

"'If you're short of something for the last couple days," he said as though she hadn't spoken, "Josh tells me Heather has a few ideas. The miniatures and something else. We might let her give them a try. See how she does. Just in case."

Tess saw red, but she struggled to keep her temper.

"If we're going to feature miniatures, don't you think it would make more sense to do it during July when we could tie it to the state convention? More of an angle," she said crisply. "Or during the county-fair competition when people might be getting tired of moo-cows?

"And let's stop pussyfooting," she said, weary now. "Am I really going to have a show next week, or am I going to get my walking papers?"

At last, the station manager sat up, regarding her with no hint of emotion.

"I've talked with our owner about you at some length today. Leah thinks your features and show are generally good, and of course she's not eager to have it said around town that she's a hardass. She says that we're to keep you for the time being—just as long as there are no more problems."

Chapter Nine

"WHITMORE?" CALLED TESS AS SHE STEPPED INTO the house, entering through the kitchen, that afternoon. "Who did the garage door?"

Whitmore sniffed.

"I did. What's the matter, didn't you think I'd know how to paint?"

"I just never expected—oh, Whitmore, I'm so grateful!" She sank down on the edge of the wing chair in the living room.

The older woman peered at her over the tops of her glasses.

"It appeared to me you could use some help. If there's anything more I can do, if you'd like to get out some evening with some friends and relax a little—"

"No. I just want to get Zach through this now." Tess choked on her words. "I don't want this to ruin his whole life, Whitmore. I want him to get over this and be happy again. He's always been such a wonderful kid!"

Whitmore touched her shoulder in passing.

"I know he is. And he's mighty lucky, with you. But you're looking worn down yourself. Just keep my offer in mind."

Tess saw her to the door. Then, as she'd done half a dozen times since Sunday, she walked over and stared at the phone. Twice before, she had gotten as far as picking it up. Today, before her courage could abandon her, she dialed the number of Andy Rowe's parents. She had to try and express her sorrow to them. She had to say—she didn't know what.

"Annette?" she said uncertainly as the phone was answered. "This is Tess Bondurant. I—"

On the other end, the phone crashed down. It left a void inside her. *Well, what did you expect?* she asked herself. If she were in Annette Rowe's place, would she be any different?

Shortly afterward, as she looked out the window, children began meandering home from school. Tess felt her chest tightening, preparing for the sight of her child dragging home in isolation again. But today, before she even glimpsed him, she heard the chant:

> *"Zachary shoots people,*
> *Zachary shoots people . . ."*

She left the door open, the need to protect bursting inside her. Half a dozen boys—the same boys who had been participants in Sunday afternoon's target play—danced backward, mocking Zach, who walked alone. Some automatic governor took over as she neared them, and she spoke calmly, restrained mostly by her unwillingness to let Zach see how upset she was.

"Sammy—Peter—that's enough!" she said as they turned, spotting her. "I must say I'm disappointed in all of you. I thought you boys understood what it meant being friends."

Not one of them answered her. Sammy drew his sneaker uneasily over the concrete.

"What happened to Zach could have happened to any of you. You all were there," she reminded. She met Zach's eyes with her own and signaled toward the house. "Come on. Let's go."

One of Zach's tormentors had already bolted across the street to his own house and scooted inside. The door opened now, and his mother stepped out, glaring at Tess.

"Maybe you should take care of your own child's behavior before you go butting in lecturing others!'' she shouted at Tess.

And to think, I kept your son overnight for a week while you were in the hospital, Tess thought bitterly. Beside her, Zach drew his shoulders up and hung his head.

Without a word exchanged, they walked up the steps and through the open front door. Then Zach looked at her with misery in his eyes.

''I'm sorry,'' he said.

''Sorry, Zach? Whatever for?'' Tess fought to maintain her pretense of calm. ''It was the others who were out of line, I'd say. How long have they been treating you like that?''

He shrugged.

''Damn it, Zachary!'' Tess's curling fist hit an empty coffee mug and sent it skidding against the kitchen faucet where it splintered. ''Don't pretend you don't know—I know you do!''

''Andy was their friend,'' he mumbled, as though that made a difference.

''Of course he was their friend—and so were you! And weren't you listening to what I said out there? Every one of those boys is just as much to blame for Andy's death as you are! I want you to get that through your head. The gun should never have been brought out in the first place, but it was, and when you happened to be the one who was holding it, Andy grabbed it. No amount of grieving's going to bring him back. So I want you to stop it. Do you hear me?''

Halting, she bit hard on her lip. She had wanted to help her child, to comfort him, and instead she was yelling.

''Okay,'' he said in a dull little voice, and before she could collect her wits, he sat down in front of the TV set and snapped on the picture.

Tess stood for a shaken moment, aware Zach never watched anything at this hour but unable to issue a reprimand. She walked with careful composure toward her bedroom, closed the door, and grateful for the noise of electronic voices to mask it, gave way to tears.

They came in great wrenching sobs that left her stomach burning. She was failing Zach, she told herself, grinding her face into the bedspread to muffle her agony. Was there something she could do beyond just worrying, just talking and listening? She knew he needed time for the healing to come, but the waiting was horrible. Maybe she wasn't doing enough. Should she go door to door? Plead with the other parents for understanding? Would it help?

She rolled over on her back, too emotionally spent now to think clearly. As she lay looking dry-eyed at the ceiling, the doorbell rang. Let Zach get it, she thought. The routine of such small tasks was probably what he needed. But no, what if it were another irate parent whose child she'd scolded? Zach shouldn't face that. Aware that her hair was disheveled, aware that her nose and cheeks were probably splotchy from crying, she drew a sleeve across the last of her tears and went to answer.

As she looked through the glass panel over the door, she saw with surprise that it was Forrest Diadazzio standing on her doorstep.

"Hello," she said, aware she sounded less than welcoming.

He smiled at her nevertheless.

"I know it's not good manners dropping by uninvited, but do you mind if I come in?"

"Of course not." She stepped aside. Zach had snapped off the TV and was on his way to the bedroom. "Zach," she said. "This is Dr. Diadazzio. His brother was a guest on my show today."

Forrest smiled at the small boy, who looked miniature beside him, and put out his hand.

"Hi, Zach. I'm Forrest."

Zach shook hands dutifully and started to turn away.

"I see you have a hermit crab," said Forrest. "So do I."

Zach, though he paused, made no comment, so Forrest spoke again.

"This one's got an awfully nice shell. What's its name?"

Zach glanced at him reluctantly.

"Herman."

"Herman the Hermit." Forrest grinned. "How about that. That's what I call mine."

Tess held her breath as something flickered on Zach's freckled face, but it was only a quizzical look, no real response, that she saw there.

"Oh," he said.

"Hey, Zach," said Forrest as he started away again. "I stopped to see if I could talk you and your mom into going to dinner with me some place. What do you think?"

Tess felt herself immediately torn in two directions. Part of her was certain she shouldn't accept this invitation. The other part watched as Zach was forced to look at her and consider an answer.

"I don't care," he said with the shrug of the shoulders she was starting to dread. This time, Forrest let him go on his way.

"Not exactly boundless enthusiasm," he said when they were alone.

"I'm sorry." Tess rubbed one sleeve, which was damp with the tears she'd wiped on it. "It was a nice offer."

"Was? Is," corrected Forrest. "I hardly expected him to turn handsprings after what he's been through. In fact, it would probably be a lot to expect that from any kid, with some strange guy turning up and horning in on things like I did." He paused a moment, considering her. "You will go, won't you? It would be good for Zach—good for both of you."

Tess struggled only briefly before capitulating. "It would be heavenly just to get Zach out of the house for a little while," she admitted. She couldn't help thinking she'd begged Bill to accomplish this exact same thing.

Forrest made himself comfortable with a paper while she excused herself to change. Zach looked at her but did not question when she stuck her head in and told him to wash his face and put on clean clothes. More time had elapsed in the course of her crying siege than she'd recognized. It was already dinner time. Sliding quickly into a shirtwaist dress of light-blue chambray, she ran a comb through her hair, then, with her hand on the doorknob, turned back for the touch of perfume that she'd all but forgotten these last few years.

"You look terrific," said Forrest when he saw her. He took her arm, and Tess felt the blood inside her veer from its orderly circulation.

It wasn't supposed to be like this, she reminded herself. Besides, they were only taking Zach to dinner.

"Apart from pancakes, which your mom tells me are your favorite, what kind of food do you like?" Forrest asked the boy when they were all in the car.

"I don't care," said Zach from his place in the back seat.

Tess had twisted slightly and could see both him and Forrest.

"Good," said Forrest. "There's a great vegetarian place not far from here. I'll bet you'd love their soybean loaf with scalloped eggplant."

Tess thought she saw a slight expression of dismay come over Zach.

"You fond of vegetables?" continued Forrest with gusto.

"Well—" Zach looked in her direction and gulped. "Not really."

Forrest kept his eyes on traffic, but Tess was almost certain she saw the corner of his mouth quirk.

"Now that I think about it, I do believe the vegetable place is closed on Thursdays," he said. "What do you say we drive into Dayton and give Charley's Crab our business?"

Though he volunteered no more comments, Zach looked around when they entered the restaurant, which was two stories up and opened onto the rotunda of a restored arcade. From their seat beside a polished brass railing, they could watch people moving down below, walking to the small shops that lined the bottom portion of the arcade. Forrest, while seeming to feel no need of constant chatter, kept a comfortable conversation going for all of them. In spite of Zach's silence, in spite of his lack of appetite, Tess was sorry to see the evening come to an end.

On the way home in the car, Zach yawned. Perhaps tonight he could fall asleep without those pills the doctor had left, Tess thought.

"I won't ask you in. I'd like to get Zach settled," she said at the door. "But thank you, Forrest. Thank you very much."

He nodded. "My pleasure."

He didn't move away, and by the way he was looking at her, Tess knew he longed to touch her. She was alarmed to feel the pressing of nerves beneath her skin that told her she also longed for that touch.

"You're very kind, doing this for a little boy you don't even know," she said, drawing her eyes out of range of his so he could not see. "You're a credit to Albert."

He smiled, but it was a sober smile. "I like Zach. And I happen to like his mother very much. I admire her grit."

He had opened the door for Zach and still held it slightly ajar. Now he released it and put both large hands gently against Tess's face.

"Good night, Tess," he said, and bending, allowed his lips just the slightest taste of hers.

He did not release her at once. They looked for some seconds into each other's eyes. And feeling the accelerated tempo of her own breathing, Tess knew that if ever they kissed again, it would not be so lightly.

Chapter Ten

IT WAS MORNING AND TESS AND KATIE WERE BRAIN storming how to edit a segment they'd shot on day care for the elderly when Tess's phone rang. As Tess answered, Katie bent to retrieve a sheet of paper from the wastebasket, study it, and shake her head.

"You're right. This garbage you were writing earlier is even worse," the camerawoman said cheerfully as Tess hung up. She stopped and peered at Tess. "What's wrong?"

"Earle wants to see me." Tess felt the words come stiffly out as she rose. "I'll bet we've lost another damn sponsor!"

Katie sent her a worried look. "I'll wait right here till you get back."

Tess knocked on the door to Earle's office, then entered without waiting. Josh was there, too, lounging easily in a chair, but it was Earle who spoke.

"Tess. This isn't pleasant. Those women from the Home and Hearth League are threatening a picket line if we don't take you off the air. Things apparently are more sensitive than we'd thought because of that show you did yesterday.

"Needless to say, the station doesn't want to be in the position of deliberately offending its viewers. We can move you back to your old job. Are you interested?"

"My old job! Do you mean production assistant?" Tess was stunned.

Beginner's work, she thought. *Beginner's pay.*

76

"At what sort of salary?" she asked coldly—coldly because that was how these men who held the power played their game.

"Well—" Earle smiled engagingly. "I'm sure we could bring it up a little from what P. T. gets."

"Do you realize I have a child to support?" Tess demanded.

Hands curling into fists, she came closer to Earle's desk. "Do you realize my son, on top of everything else he has to feel guilty about, will blame himself if you—if I—" She made a mute gesture. "And what about P. T.? Will you keep her on the payroll if I step down?"

Josh, tamping tobacco into his pipe, gave a cynical look at Earle, who seemed unperturbed.

"I doubt the budget could take that, Tess," he said amiably. "And you have seniority—"

"No! I will not step down." Tess could feel the heat in her cheeks. "You want me to spare the station any hint of nastiness, don't you? Well, it's not going to work! If you want to get rid of me, you're going to have to fire me— and everyone's damn sure going to know it! This is absurd. We've got viewers besides the Home and Hearth League. What kind of people are you, what kind of ethics— what kind of *hearts* do you have—to not even make a pretense of backing someone who's—who's—"

She couldn't finish. She didn't know how. "Someone who's one of your own," she'd started to say, but she wasn't sure now she'd ever been that. Perhaps she'd only thought she was.

"It's almost time for me to go meet a guest," she said. Squaring her shoulders, she walked out.

"Well?" asked Katie when she returned.

Tess told her.

"Shit," said Katie. She shook her head. "I can see why people join a union."

"You know what?" Tess fumbled angrily through her purse. "I've never believed it before, but I'm starting to think it's the people who'll put a knife in someone's back who get ahead. Maybe it's just not possible to survive and be a good person. Maybe you have to choose between being stepped on and being a stepper.''

"The fact you're just now seeing all that just shows what an innocent you've been to date,'' Katie said dryly.

Tess blew her nose with vigor. "Excuse me. I've got to go look cute or bright or whatever.'' Her laugh was uneven. "Do you know one of Zach's little friends told him last week that I must be a star? I'll bet you never knew I moved in such a glamorous milieu!''

The show that morning went slowly, and Tess knew it was her fault. Little by little, at work and when she faced her child and neighborhood in the evening, her energy was being siphoned away. As soon as she was off the air, she left with a cameraman to do a short feature on a man who made hand-operated bookbinding presses. Even if they'd let Heather take her place temporarily, she'd be wise to justify her place on the payroll, wouldn't she?

Four hours later, she was done for the day. She had called to make an appointment to see Zach's teacher. It meant she would not be there when he returned from school, but Tess felt it was important to learn whether he was being as shunned and heckled in classes as he had been walking home from school the previous day. Whitmore would be watching to make sure that didn't happen again, she thought grimly.

Zach's teacher, as though embarrassed by Tess's presence, seemed preoccupied with the rearrangement of her desk as they talked. No, Zach wasn't being harassed, she said. Well, there had been a comment or two, but of course she'd intervened.

And how was he interacting with the other children?

She opened a bottle of rubber cement, peered into it, and replaced the cap.

Frankly, they were ignoring him, having only whatever contact was required with him in class. And at recess, on the playground, he was alone.

The woman looked at Tess directly and took a breath. Her expression was kind.

"Speaking candidly, Mrs. Bondurant, I think the fact you're something of a celebrity, and that the other children therefore hear their parents talking about you, makes all this harder on Zach. If you weren't in the public eye, this might be forgotten more quickly. I realize it's asking a lot and that a leave of absence is probably difficult to arrange, but—well—Zach's a wonderful child. My heart aches for him. Perhaps you could put his welfare first—just for the time being?"

Tess smarted beneath the polite criticism. You've put your own needs, yes, your ego first, it implied. Then she realized she was being unfair. The woman across the desk from her had meant to be helpful.

Was it ego that was making her cling so tenaciously to her job? *Had* she put her own interests ahead of her son's? But no, it was Zach himself who had felt that deep need to return to school, and sometimes it was necessary to confront fears to expunge them.

The teacher was wrong. She meant well, and Tess was grateful for her concern and the courage that it must have taken for her to speak out, but she hadn't been through all these questions a hundred times as Tess had.

"I wish it were as simple as that," she said ruefully. Rising, she held out her hand. "Thank you for your time. And for being honest. If there's any problem—anything you think I should know about—please let me know."

As she walked down the corridor of the school, Tess could feel the teacher's eyes on her. In spite of her reassurances to herself, doubts flooded her. *Was* she doing the right thing by Zach continuing this fight? Maybe she should step down to a lower job. Or move.

When she got home, Whitmore was working a crossword puzzle. She nodded her gray head toward the back door. Through the kitchen window Tess could see Zach huddled on the small concrete slab that passed for a porch, his eyes fixed on two of his friends playing catch in the yard next door.

"Been there for half an hour," said Whitmore. "Poor mite."

When Whitmore had gone, Tess poured herself a mug of coffee. Pulling her features into an expression of unconcern, she went out and sat beside Zach.

"Hi. How was school?" she said.

"Okay."

She was used to the monosyllables now. Could this be the child who used to weary her ears with his chatter?

"Want to go to the pancake house for supper?"

"No."

The answer, as well as the decisiveness of his tone, surprised her. Even Forrest's invitation last night had drawn only passive indifference.

Tess frowned at him.

"Why not?"

"Just don't." He turned and fixed her with a hard little look. "Andy's funeral's tomorrow. I want to go."

Coffee spilled on Tess's arm, but she didn't look down. The lump produced by his unhidden suffering was choking her.

"Oh, Zach—"

"I want to go, Mom. If I go, maybe Andy's mom will understand I'm sorry."

Tess was silent. She squeezed his hand. "We'll go."

She thought she felt him sigh inaudibly and lean toward her. God, now what sort of corner had she backed herself into, she wondered, remembering that receiver slamming down when she'd called Annette Rowe.

"Want to play some Monopoly?" she asked after an interval.

Zach shook his head.

"I wish Dad'd had time to play catch with the new glove he brought," he volunteered when another silence had come and gone.

"I'll play catch with you," Tess said.

He regarded her soberly for a moment. "Thanks. But you're not much good. It was just a dumb idea, anyway. It's okay."

He settled his chin on his knees, and Tess, after a few minutes more, concluded she could only leave him to his unhappiness. Going back inside, she drank the coffee and thought about Zach's teacher.

"Well, damn it, maybe I *have* let pride get in my way," she said to the empty kitchen. Before she could change her mind, she went to the phone and called Bill.

He was at work, of course, and not pleased at the interruption. Tess had never done this before, come to him asking help. She got to the point at once.

"Bill. I need to talk to you. Please. It's about Zach and—everything. It's very important."

She could hear him hesitate and then speak grudgingly. "I suppose you mean today. All right. I'll try to get away early and come over."

When she hung up, Tess debated tactics. Should she make Bill the cocktail he always liked after work? Somehow that seemed uncomfortably intimate—as though they were still man and wife. Yet she wanted to avoid those unproductive arguments they always seemed to have, so in the end she did.

He was peering at his watch when she answered the door, a pointed hint to her, she felt certain.

"God, I can use this," he said with surprise when she gave him the drink. He took a deep swallow, then stretched his legs out comfortably in front of him. "Okay, Tess." He cocked an eyebrow at her. "What's this about?"

Tess sat uneasily on the edge of her own chair.

"Bill, if I—if I were to lose my job at the station, would you be able to help us out financially? Just for a few months?"

His relaxed posture vanished, and he sat upright.

"Do you think that's going to *happen*?"

The horror in his voice told her what she needed to know.

"It might. Things don't look good. And it might take me a while to find something else."

He drank quickly from the glass in his hand and set it aside.

"I'd help where I could, Tess. You know that. But I've got a lot of expenses. A hell of a lot. And don't forget, you *are* the one who wanted the divorce."

So much for swallowing pride and turning to Bill for help, Tess thought.

"Of course," she said. "Well, that's one thing. The other is that I thought you might take Zach somewhere for a bite. He turned me down when I suggested the pancake house, but you're more of a novelty—"

Bill bridled. "If that's what you called me over here for, to criticize—"

"Oh, Bill, for heaven's sakes! I didn't mean it that way. I only meant that he responds to you sometimes when he doesn't to me. And he—he said this afternoon he wished that he could see you."

It was a small lie. Bill seemed pacified now. He looked almost guiltily at his hands.

"Let me make a phone call," he said, so subdued now that Tess felt almost sorry for him. He disappeared into the kitchen where she could hear him speaking in lowered tones, no doubt to Caroline.

A few moments later, the back door opened and closed and opened again. Zach walked beside his father, his expression considerably less enthusiastic than it could have been, Tess thought with a small worry. Well, surely Bill understood that even apart from this present crisis it was hard dealing with a parent who no longer was a day-to-day constant in your life. She listened to the two of them leave in Bill's car, then sat down on the couch, suddenly aware she had a pounding headache.

She had fallen asleep on the couch when she heard the knock on the door. As she sat up, Tess saw by the clock on one wall that barely an hour had passed.

It alarmed her when she saw Bill standing on the other side of the door. As she opened it, Zach stomped past.

"That kid needs to see a shrink. He's well on his way to being autistic or something," Bill said before she could speak.

Tess pulled the door shut so Zach couldn't hear. "That's what I've been trying to tell you. He—"

"He doesn't talk, he doesn't show interest in anything, he doesn't even appear to eat these days—though that part might have been different if I hadn't been forced to deal with him right after he'd been dragged along with this Forrest whoever." Bill's dark eyes flashed at her in accusation. "I'm telling you, Tess, the kid's got problems. He needs to see a therapist."

He had unearthed her deepest-seated fears. Tess gripped the side of the door, resisting them.

"He needs patience! He needs *your help*, Bill!"

"Me? What makes you think I can help him?"

"You're his father, for God's sake!"

They eyed each other. Bill's voice was brittle.

"He needs to leave this neighborhood."

Tess flung her hands up in utter frustration.

"You don't solve problems by running away from them, Bill."

As he drew himself rigid, she realized he thought she was alluding to him—to the stream of jobs that had never quite panned out. Well, maybe in some subconscious way she had been.

"I see no point in prolonging this conversation," Bill said, and walked away.

Tess had managed to lock herself out. By the time she had pressed the bell and hammered on the door enough to bring Zach, Bill was gone.

Zach let her in without comment. Returning to his room, he flung himself face down across the bed. Although she was uncertain how much to press him, Tess nonetheless finally went in and sat down beside him. Needing contact, longing to console, she stroked back his hair.

"Not a very good outing, huh?" she ventured.

"Dad got mad at me," he said, voice muffled.

Tess thought quickly. "I think he's been having some sort of little tiff with Caroline."

He didn't answer, but Tess felt him snuggle against her hand where it rested on him.

"It's pretty tough for you, isn't it, Zach? Your teacher tells me the kids at school aren't being very nice to you."

"They don't like me," he said in that same muffled voice. Then, after a small pause, he said, "It's okay."

How could she answer him? Perhaps Bill had been right when he'd said Zach needed professional help.

They remained there for a long time before Zach turned over on his back and looked at her. His lower lip trembled.

"I miss Dad," he said. "I mean—" He struggled for words or control; she didn't know which. "You're great, Mom, the best mom ever, but sometimes I feel like you're the only one who really likes me."

Tess turned her head so he wouldn't see the sparkle of tears.

Miles distant, in the living room, the phone intruded. Tess answered and recognized Forrest's voice.

"How are you doing?" he asked.

Tess sighed. The man must have some fascination with misery to initiate contact in this period of their lives.

"Oh, things are getting a little better, I think," she said without believing it.

"That's good. Could I talk to Zach?"

"Of course." The request caught her off guard. She returned to Zach's bedroom. "It's Forrest—from last night. He'd like to talk to you."

Looking as surprised as she was, Zach slipped from the bed.

"Well?" she said when he returned.

He shrugged. "He asked me what my favorite kind of ice cream was. I said Superman. He said, well, his was chocolate almond, so he'd bring both."

"He's coming over? Now?"

"I guess."

A smile raised the corner of Tess's lips and her spirits as well. It was crazy, but she blessed Forrest for the craziness. At least Zach was willing to state a preference in ice creams!

Forrest arrived ten minutes later, a sack in hand.

"Hi. Have the bowls out?" he asked in greeting. "Hello, Zach. I thought we needed some cookies, so I put a box of those in, too. Will you please enlighten me? What's Superman ice cream?"

"It's like his cape," said Zach as they moved toward the kitchen. "It's blue and red and yellow swirled together."

"Tastes every bit as atrocious as it sounds." Tess laughed.

"Does not."

"Well, I hope you like it a lot because I have a feeling you're going to have half a gallon to eat all by yourself," Forrest warned.

"The other dentists in town should run you out for dealing this much sugar," Tess teased. She filled their bowls and brought them to the table.

Zach shoveled a bite of the sky-blue ice cream into his mouth.

"Is that what you do?" he asked. "Are you a dentist?"

"Well, sort of like. I take out teeth that get stuck underneath and can't come out. I stitch up people who've gotten hit in the mouth with a baseball bat—like that."

"Sounds dull." Zach spooned more Superman into his mouth and looked at Forrest with newly hostile eyes. "My dad designs airplanes. He knows the astronauts."

For the first time since the accident, Tess wanted to slug him. He was being deliberately bratty, and he was certainly showing his father's own flair for stretching the truth. Bill's company was currently working on some minor contract for NASA. Bill had been to the space center twice and, yes, had probably met some of the astronauts. It had made him a hero in his son's eyes, and Tess felt certain Bill had embellished the story. Now Zach appeared to have conveniently forgotten how, come Christmas and birthday, his father had failed to deliver the autographed picture of one of the famous spacemen that he'd promised.

"That sounds exciting," said Forrest with a generous smile.

Zach was crunching down a cookie now and didn't answer. This was the most interest he'd shown in anything since Sunday, Tess thought. She got up to bring the coffee, which had not been ready when they sat down, turning back just in time to witness what happened next.

For some reason she could not fathom, Zach had risen on his knees. He reached across now to touch the pocket of Forrest's shirt. Forrest, who was looking down at his bowl, jerked back, shoving Zach's hand aside.

"Hey, what are you doing?" he demanded sharply.

Tess froze. Zach's face had gone white.

"I—I just wanted to see what that thing in your pocket was," he said.

Tess couldn't believe this. Forrest didn't seem like the type to worry about his shirt getting smudged by a child's hands. He glanced down and tossed something shiny onto the table.

"Oh, that. It's just a dental pick. I took it home to work on a little calculator I have that's broken. There, you can look at it if you want."

His words were tight. He looked at Tess uncomfortably and then at Zach.

"Look, I'm sorry I growled. You startled me. Still friends?"

Zach nodded and went back to eating ice cream, this time in silence. Slightly mystified, Tess joined them. The episode had shaken her. She smiled at Forrest uneasily. Apparently, under his calm exterior, there were tensions, just as in anyone else.

When the doorbell rang a short time later, she was almost relieved.

"Zach, will you please?" she asked.

A moment later, Katie and her husband, Leroy, came in.

"Do you by any chance rent kids to take to movies?" Katie asked. "We're going to some creepy science-fiction thing and need our hands held. Oh." She stopped as she saw Forrest sitting at the kitchen table. "We've barged in, haven't we?"

"Not a bit. Want some ice cream?" He rose for introductions.

In the bedlam that ensued, Katie whispered in Tess's ear that they'd seen the movie and that it contained no violence and, more important, no guns. Zach, though displaying his all-too-frequent indifference, finally acknowledged he supposed he'd like to go.

"May stop for a burger afterwards, but we'll have him home by midnight," Katie said. " 'By."

"Ah," said Forrest when Tess came back into the kitchen. "Just the two of us and a gallon of ice cream—half of it blue."

Tess laughed. "I don't think I've eaten ice cream for supper since I was a kid. I must apologize for Zach's behavior, by the way. I'm afraid he had a clash with his father earlier. He's not usually so rude."

In spite of their lightness, the atmosphere in the kitchen had suddenly changed. She was very much aware of Forrest's presence. She was very much aware of him as a man. After her divorce, she had gone out with a few men, but this was different. Perhaps it was only her heightened sense of the two of them alone in the house.

"No problem. At least his appetite's okay," said Forrest mildly. "Things must be chaotic if this was supper. I take it there are stresses apart from Zach?"

There was a quality about him that made it easy to talk. Tess found herself telling him about the graffiti, about the neighbors' children taunting Zach, about the mother's sharp words to Tess when she interfered.

"It's guilt on their parts. And fear," he said. "That sneaking realization it could have been their kid on the spot instead of Zach. Confronting that's too scary. It's easier to attack, pretend they could never be in your place.''

Her smile was tired. ''That's what I've thought sometimes, but I've been half afraid it was only rationalization.''

He reached across the table and touched her hand.

''You know what I think, Tess? I think it would do you a world of good to get out for a while. Let's go for a drive.''

Tess sat motionless, feeling the full force of his eyes, feeling the light touch of his finger tips. Something inside her trembled. She felt vulnerable. A small prickling on the surface of her skin warned her that anything was wiser than continuing to sit here like this.

''We'd be back by midnight—eleven-thirty in case Zach's early,'' he said.

She drew her hand free, aware of the rub of flesh on flesh, and nodded.

Chapter Eleven

As they rode along, Tess recognized that their conversation had grown stilted. Her headache had also returned. She pressed her temple.

"I've seen you do that several times," said Forrest. "Headache?"

"Yes."

I'm a hell of a date, thought Tess, *but then this really isn't a date. Forrest surely knows that. He's just being kind. And maybe he's a little lonely. That's all.*

"It's tension," he said. "Well, in that case, instead of stopping in at some bar, I'll take you to my place. It's a veritable pleasure palace, complete with Jacuzzi. Great for unwinding. That's what you need."

Tess's breathing halted. Panic stirred. This was not what she wanted—not what she had expected. And she felt disappointed that Forrest would make this kind of move.

He glanced at her as though aware of her silence, then looked deliberately straight ahead.

"Look, Tess, I won't pretend that I don't want to make love to you—that I haven't wanted to since I saw you standing there all small and desperate and ready to take on Albert and the whole damn world if necessary. From the little I know, you've got qualities I consider fairly rare in a woman—rare in anyone. But I've got sense enough to know the time's all wrong. You're carrying a pretty heavy load. And so—" His smile was rueful. "It really was a perfectly innocent invitation. You can lock yourself in. Have all the privacy you want.''

In a way, his utter honesty was more disturbing to Tess than her first assumption had been. She twisted the stem of her watch, almost too embarrassed to speak. He wanted to take her to bed. He was blunt about that. But she also believed she would be completely safe with him.

She drew a sharp breath, an unexpected feeling stabbing at her groin. Just for an instant, she found herself wondering what it would be like to have this large man with the strong, gentle hands make love to her.

Her pulse was racing, and that was completely ridiculous. He was open; he'd made an offer out of compassion, and if she refused, she would join the ranks of those who put down both those qualities.

''Thank you,'' she said at last.

His ''place'' was a graystone house two stories high, set outside of town on a road lined with small farms whose fields were just now being plowed. It had been a farmhouse, Forrest explained as he led the way through a front door trimmed by white paint whose glistening freshness was just perceivable in the darkness, but a neighbor had bought the tillable land, and the house and two acres of woods had been just the sort of place he'd been hunting.

Inside, the rooms were high ceilinged and simply furnished and gave an impression of space adequate to Forrest's size. The floors were oak and beautifully maintained. The furnishings were a startling mix of expensive modern upholstered pieces and antique tables.

''The spot for relaxing's through that door,'' said Forrest, pointing. ''You can lock yourself in since you don't have a suit. The woman who does my laundry and housework keeps some robes done up for me if you want one. Take your time, and if you're interested afterwards, I'll have something ready to drink.''

He disappeared toward another part of the house, and Tess stood looking into what was obviously part of a later addition. It was one step down from the living area and floored in stone, and there, amid tubbed plants and natural wood, was a sunken Jacuzzi easily large enough to accommodate four people.

She shook her head in mild amazement. Somehow she would never have pictured Forrest as the type to invite people over for cocktails in the whirlpool. Yet as she admired the skylight above and the glass wall in back that must give a spectacular view of the woods by daylight, a sensation of delighted hedonism crept through her.

"Which only proves you can't tell a thing about a man by the way he looks," she said beneath her breath.

Well, she was here, and she'd never had the opportunity to experience one of these luxurious toys before. With only a twinge of uncertainty, she reached behind her and locked the door, then turned on the water.

As it jetted out, she walked quickly to close the shutters across the glass wall. She left her clothes in the small dressing room that occupied one corner. Just as she'd been told, there were fresh terry-cloth robes stacked on one corner of the vanity. She took one with her and walked out and down the steps into the water.

Pleasure palace is right, she thought, sitting back on one of the built-in benches and closing her eyes with a sigh. This was better than a bath, better than a swimming pool. The water swirling out on every side of her massaged her gently. Half opening her eyes, she looked at the greenery of the plants, smelled the sweet, damp stones around her. This was a haven. This was a different world— and all of a sudden she burst into tears.

Cascading down her cheeks, they lost themselves in the water caressing her shoulders. Dumb, Tess told herself as she tried to restrain them. Totally dumb. Here she was in a glorious spot with a chance to forget her worries, and instead, in the first moment that she relaxed, they came to the surface. She hiccuped, catching her breath raggedly as emotion rushed out of her. Then, discarding the struggle and blind to the exotic room, she let herself weep.

She wept because she was all Zach had and she wasn't sure she was getting through to him.

She wept because confronted with that frozen world in which he'd locked himself, she'd only managed to make small cracks.

All right. You had to face your problems head-on if you wanted to solve them, not run. But she thought she'd done that with Zach, and he, poor little guy, seemed to make heroic efforts in that vein, too. She'd tried to set a pattern of normality for him. She was trying as hard as she dared to lead him gently back to things and activities he'd once liked. If he wouldn't talk, she at least had reassured him again and again that he hadn't been responsible for Andy's death; if he couldn't sort out his own feelings, she at least had coaxed him to share some, as he had in that horrible outburst yesterday. In spite of all of it, progress seemed almost nonexistent. What if it wasn't enough? What more could she do?

Slowly, the long, fierce rush of emotion subsided. Exhausted by this act of letting down, she lay back and splashed water over her face. She felt calmer now. Her efforts with Zach seemed drawn into sharper focus, ready to tackle afresh. Her time in this room had hardly been spent in the way Forrest must have envisioned, yet it had soothed her.

Time passed. She felt her eyelids drooping with a strange lethargy and jerked her head up quickly. She had better not linger. She had no idea what hour it was getting to be.

When she got out, the very effort of movement felt too much to make. She wrapped herself in the swaddling white robe, glad to postpone, for the moment, the task of getting into clothes. A look at the watch she'd left in the dressing room told her it still was early. There was time for that drink Forrest had offered, and with her headache surprisingly gone, she found herself in the mood.

Tess hesitated. Should she dress first? The mere thought of it marred this sense of catharsis that she felt now. The robe she was wearing covered her like a burnoose, its belt

92

long enough to encircle her waist two times. She tied it securely and unlocked the door into the living room.

"Ah-hah. I was just about to yell and make sure you hadn't drowned," said Forrest, coming in from what was obviously the kitchen and catching sight of her. He handed her one of the large-stemmed goblets he was carrying. "Here, this is just what you need to round out the evening."

She saw what the glasses held at the same time she felt its heat on her fingers.

"Warm milk?" she asked, wrinkling her nose in disbelief.

"With just a touch of vanilla. Great for headaches. Great for teeth. Say, maybe that's why you have headaches—something wrong in there. Let's see."

He pressed a finger on her lower incisors, opening her mouth and squinting inside with one eye.

"Well, doctor?" She gave a tired smile, though with his finger still in her mouth, that proved difficult.

He grinned. "Don't ask me. I can't tell a thing without x-rays." With what must be professional expertise at moving chins, he tipped hers toward the light. "You've been crying in there, haven't you? Your eyes are red."

Expelling a sigh, Tess sat down on the couch.

"I have a problem with Zach—not wanting his mind to be messed up by what's happened to him. The trouble is, I don't know if I'm handling it very well or whether what he really needs is professional help."

Forrest made no move to join her. He stood above her, slowly rotating the contents of the glass in his hand.

"Albert says the parents can do more to help a child than anyone else if they're willing."

Smiling felt easier now. She nodded. "I guess that's what I've been telling myself."

Ducking her head, Tess took a drink of milk. She felt Forrest settling easily on the couch beside her.

"There are things I'm taking as hopeful signs," she said. "He cried his heart out the other day, and I felt he needed to do that—to admit his grief. And I got him to talk about how he was feeling." She shuddered. "That was horrible. Sometimes he seems to be responding a little—he did tonight about the ice cream—but—''

She set her glass down on a nearby table with a crack.

''But damn it, then he seems to draw right back within himself. I coax, and I prod, and—sometimes I find myself wondering if he *enjoys* being miserable! He won't get mad at the other kids for shunning him. He tortures himself sitting and watching them play. Sometimes I get so furious with him I could—I don't know what. I ought to be understanding, and instead I turn around and yell at him.''

''You some kind of candidate for sainthood that you can't get angry?'' asked Forrest reasonably. ''Most people yell.''

For a second, she felt irritation that he could dismiss it so lightly. Then she knew that he was absolutely right.

''I know,'' she said. ''And I think I am making progress.'' Pushing up the sleeve of her robe, she checked her watch.

Forrest touched her shoulder very gently.

''Relax, Tess. How was the Jacuzzi?''

''Heavenly. It really was.'' She thought of her watch, though.

His hand massaged her collarbone as though aware of her tension.

''I'll keep track of the time. I promise. Trust me.''

Tess looked at him, realizing how much, after such a short acquaintance, she did trust him. When she was in his presence, she could feel herself warming in it as though before an open fire, turning to him, toward the brightness.

''Something the matter?'' he asked. ''You look uneasy.''

She shook her head. ''No, everything's lovely. It's just—'' She drew a breath. ''It's been a long time since I've been with anyone like this, I guess.''

God, how euphemistic could you get, she thought? She'd made it sound worse than she'd meant. Annoyed, and conscious now of his arm on the couch behind her, she looked around.

''I don't see your hermit crab,'' she said.

He was silent a moment until her gaze came back and met his.

"That's probably because I don't have one," he said slowly. "And if you're wondering why I told Zach I did, I suppose it's because I thought it was something that might draw him out. And, I might as well admit it, because I wanted him to like me."

The answer sparked twin responses in Tess: uneasiness that he would tell a lie to win Zach's approval, yet pleasure, which she quickly discounted, that it would matter to him.

"For whatever it's worth to redeem me," he said, "I had intended to get one. To make it less of a fib and just in case the two of you were ever over here."

Tess hid an impulse to frown. Forrest was puzzling. Sometimes he seemed almost too good to believe, yet she was starting to see there was a strangeness about him, too. Witness this small untruth, however motivated. And there was the way he'd thrust Zach away at the table tonight.

She shook the thoughts away from her and told him about Zach's request to go to the funeral. He agreed with her cautious hope that it might prove to be some sort of turning point for Zach. Then, in a welcome switch to lighter topics, he began to tell the first of several stories about what Albert had been like when they were boys.

Eventually, the stories ended. Tess sat smiling at him. She had shifted, and the strong warmth of his hand lay against her neck. Had she been aware of it? Yes, she admitted. She thought how well this large house, with its open rooms, suited his large build and open manner. She found herself remembering the feel of his lips on hers the night before.

"Well, I guess I'd better get dressed," she said.

He didn't look at his watch. "I guess you had."

Still she didn't move. She sensed herself teetering in some precarious balance. She liked the feel of his hand, wanted it as she'd wanted no touch since Bill's. She swallowed, and Forrest's arm eased around her shoulder. He shifted closer, and she raised her mouth to his.

A longing like no other she'd ever known flowed through

her, a longing to be part of this man and make him part of her. He was strong, and she touched his cheek, marveling at his gentleness. The movement of his hands along the rough cloth of her robe excited her. He tipped her head back, stretching her body straighter before his. She opened her mouth to him as his hand moved up to brush her breast.

Sensations. She had forgotten sensations like these existed. And she had never known them like this, tangled so tightly with something else. When his hand moved to the sash securing her robe, she made no protest. He nuzzled it gently aside, and his mouth touched her breast.

Tess gasped as pleasure mingled with pain. The room around her became a pinwheel, slowly spinning. She caught his head and held it to her hungrily.

It's right, she thought thickly. *There's something completely right about the two of us. I want that completeness. I want to wake up in his arms.*

Then, as though caught in a shroud of ice, she remembered Zach.

Abruptly and with shaking hands, she pushed away. What could she have been thinking of? How could she even be sitting here feeling—this?

Forrest's hands were on her hips now, insistent. She seized them.

"No, please!" She twisted aside. "I don't know what—" She sat up and caught her head in her hands, the robe clutched awkwardly closed with one elbow. "I'm sorry."

"Not half as sorry as I am," he said after a long delay. The words were accusing; she had been the one to encourage, and they both knew it. He picked up their empty glasses, keeping his back toward her. "I think it's probably time I took you home."

They drove back without speaking. Tess felt new misery joining the old. The evening, which could have cheered her, had ended badly, all of it her fault. And come tomorrow morning, she had to face Andy's funeral.

Chapter Twelve

"Y OU DON'T SUPPOSE I INTENDED TO LET THE TWO OF you go alone, do you?" asked Whitmore the following morning. She stood on Tess's doorstep, an unexpected visitor, just minutes before Tess and her son were ready to leave.

Tess gave her arm a quick squeeze.

"Oh, Whitmore, you did more than enough calling Mrs. Rowe to see if she'd mind our being there. You're wonderful."

"You must have caught her in a bad moment," said Whitmore. "She didn't sound anything more than a little strained when I asked, and lord knows, I expect she's feeling that toward everyone now."

Tess knew she should be reassured, but she wasn't. Facing Annette Rowe today, if that happened, would be the most difficult thing she'd ever been forced to do.

She dropped her eyes in a worried glance at Zach, who stood beside her. He had not spoken since breakfast, and his face was as pale and as set as stone.

"I do think his father might have lent a little support today." Whitmore sniffed, following her gaze.

Tess couldn't think of an answer. She had slept very little, tormented by the ordeal ahead and by the stupidity of her blunder the night before.

Whatever had made her lose control of herself like that? She frowned and slid behind the steering wheel, locked in her thoughts. It was sex, raw and simple, she told herself bitterly. Then she reconsidered. If it had been pure biological craving, it would have affected her a year—two years—ago. No, what she had felt last night had been an age-old mating urge that had at its core something more meaningful than the need for procreation, something more complex and more lasting than the need for physical release.

But how could this even be crossing her mind now, she wondered guiltily? How could she even be thinking of herself with Zach about to go through the ordeal ahead? She had tried again that morning to dissuade him from this idea. He certainly faced things more head-on than his father had, and she supposed she ought to feel some sort of gratitude for that.

Instead, she found it hard to blink back tears at the sight of him, so stiff and determined and old beyond his years, in a suit that was growing too small for him. It seemed like only yesterday he had given up dragging around a one-eared rabbit and sucking his thumb. Reaching across the seat, she squeezed his knee in reassurance. Just a week ago, he would have complained: "Aw, Mom! Cut out the baby stuff." Today he was silent.

Tess had planned for them to arrive not too late, but late enough to avoid viewing Andy's body in its small casket. She'd meant to go in to work a few hours this afternoon since she was falling behind. Now she rejected the thought. Zach needed her.

Let Heather get all the gold stars she wants, Tess thought without spirit. *Maybe people know what they're talking about when they say women with families can't keep their minds entirely on their jobs. At this exact moment, I don't care about my job as much as I do about Zach.*

Then they were at the funeral home. She and Zach and Whitmore left the car. As they crossed the parking lot, a married couple got out of another car and looked icily through them. Neighbors. Tess watched Whitmore's jaw tighten.

If we make it through this, it's all downhill.

My litany, thought Tess. My hope.

Someone else—a woman—met her face to face without betraying recognition. As they stepped inside, another woman glanced at them and whispered to her companion. Tess felt Zach shrink against her, and her stomach began to burn. But she knew his must feel worse, and it was too late to back out now.

Again, she stole a look at him, searching for some expression, some shifting of posture that might hold a clue to what he was feeling. At least she could see now, from where they stood in the front hall of the funeral home, that Andy's family would be seated in a small room off one side of the main room. She and Zach would not have to face them, not yet.

Then, before she could gather herself to walk in to where the pews were, a large hand reached from behind and toward Zach's shoulder.

It drew back abruptly, just short of touching. A voice spoke almost curtly.

"Hi, Zach."

Unable to believe it, Tess looked up into Forrest's tightly guarded face. His expression told her he had not forgotten last night.

His eyes had moved to Zach now, and some emotion showed there that Tess could not identify. They seemed to devour him, to draw Zach to him. Yet, at the same time, they seemed stiff and guarded.

"I thought you might like somebody with you," he said, avoiding her gaze. "Let's go in."

Shifting, he put Zach safely between the two of them. But why had he avoided touching her son? Tess wondered, hurt. She was confused by Forrest and by his presence here.

At the moment, though, she was most concerned about Zach. What would be his reaction? As closely as she studied him, she could not tell.

On the other side of her, Whitmore pressed her arm in

reassurance. Tess was acutely aware of the four of them, an island, with people around them looking at her and her child. Had Andy's family seen them come in? What must they be thinking? As a soloist stepped into view and a minister opened his Bible, new thoughts flashed into her brain: How would Andy's death be described? What if bringing Zach here was a blunder? What if this experience caused him to break down completely?

Reaching down, she took his hand in hers. It was cold and motionless. The minister was speaking now. The awful finality of what had happened Sunday came home afresh. Tess's throat filled with tears of selfish gratitude that Zach sat beside her, whole and alive. Yet, in a frightening way, he was not whole; looking at him, she saw that this ritual that she had hoped might work some miracle for him did not appear to be affecting him in the least.

It didn't work, she thought with a dull ache an eternity later. The service was over. The filled pews started to empty. Zach, turning to leave, was as silent as when he'd come in. His chin had not trembled once. His eyes had not flickered.

"Thank goodness," murmured Whitmore. "The family's gone out the side way—not standing in front greeting people. I've never liked that part, even in the best of times."

Tess nodded. Her attention was fixed so firmly on Zach, on steering him through the crowd, on assuring he was not jostled by hostile adults, that she almost failed to see Bill.

"Oh," she said. Then, realizing it sounded foolish, she said, "You came."

He stood just inside the entrance, his eyes traveling from her to Forrest.

"I thought I should. But I got here late—had to sit in back."

Forrest had continued out the door with Whitmore. Zach followed them, but Tess had caught the movement of his eyes, which told her he'd seen his father.

"Would you like to give Zach a ride home?" she

offered. She saw Bill waver. The set of his jaw suggested displeasure, but he controlled whatever it was that was gnawing at him.

"I'd better not. I'm supposed to be putting in some overtime this morning, to tell you the truth. Here, though. Here's a little something for him when he's feeling up to it."

Thrusting a box into her hands, he turned and disappeared out the door.

Well, couldn't you have given it to him yourself? Couldn't you have spent two minutes with him? she wondered, annoyed. Lifting the lid of the box, she saw a digital watch with a built-in video game, certain to win a child the envy of his friends—provided he had any friends to whom to display it.

"Hey, fella, you really hit the jackpot," she said as she joined her son and Whitmore in the car. "Look what Dad brought you."

Zach took the box but didn't even look inside.

The funeral must have stirred some feelings. Best to try and tap them now, Tess decided.

"That was hard," she said as they drove along. "But I'm glad we went. It felt sort of like saying good-by to Andy." She paused. "What about you, Zach?"

He shrugged.

In the rear-view mirror, Whitmore caught her eye, signaling her not to press any further. Whitmore had raised four children, and Tess respected her wisdom. She let the matter drop.

When she pulled into the drive, she was surprised to see Forrest waiting on the front step. He came forward to meet them.

"I just stopped by to give Zach this game I happened to see in the drugstore this morning," he said. "You ever have one of these things before, Zach?"

For a moment, Tess felt a twinge of something unpleasant. *Just like Bill,* she thought. *Bringing gifts.* She was surprised by her own negative reaction. It was a thoughtful gesture, after all.

Forrest had stooped and was showing his find to Zach. The game was a plastic half-dome in which a dozen metal balls rolled elusively around the slight depressions meant to hold them. Tess was sure Zach must have had such a toy at some time, but he'd shaken his head at Forrest's question. Out of lack of interest? Because the funeral had been as hard on him as she'd feared? She gave him a worried glance.

Forrest was explaining patiently: "You have to get the balls in the holes, see? All of them. Albert and I used to have a lot of fun with things like these."

"Albert?" Zach looked at him with a flicker of interest.

"That's my brother. It's really easy to get him riled up. He'd spend maybe ten or fifteen minutes working on one of these things, and just when he had one ball to go and was just about to get it, I'd bump his arm. Then he'd punch me." Forrest grinned.

"Oh," said Zach. He didn't smile.

"Is that how your nose got broken?" Tess asked to make up for the lack of response.

Forrest looked startled.

"No. That was just one of those childhood accidents," he said shortly.

He stood up. Did Tess only imagine something closed in his manner?

She lowered her voice. "Forrest, I'm sorry about last night—"

Whitmore had unlocked the door, and the phone was ringing.

"Tess, it's for you," she called. "The studio."

Annoyed, Tess brushed at the air. Couldn't she even be allowed half a minute to sort things out? Couldn't anything ever go right?

"Tess?" It was P. T.'s voice, and she sounded cautious. "Katie wasn't quite sure if you were coming in this afternoon, but I thought you should know—the guest you'd scheduled for Monday's 'Tess and Guests' just called and canceled. She didn't give a reason.''

Tess made a fist and pressed it against the wall above the phone table.

''Thanks for letting me know,'' she said. ''I guess I will come in.''

She hung up and made a grimace.

''The guest for my Monday show just canceled. These are truly the times that try women's souls.''

''I could get you an oral surgeon as a replacement,'' volunteered Forrest. He had followed her into the living room. They were alone.

''Thanks, but I expect there's a rule against it. If you can't have two spots on animals in the same week, I doubt you can have two Diadazzios.'' Her smile was fleeting, and she took a breath. ''About last night. I know I owe you an apology. I led you on. I wanted to—I guess I lost my head for a while. And then, all of a sudden, I remembered Zach.'' She cast around for words to express all she was feeling. ''I really can't thank you enough for being with us this morning.''

He gave her a dry look, and it seemed to break some barrier between them.

''Well, I had a hell of a time getting to sleep because of you, I'll grant you that. But I guess I should have had sense enough to realize—''

He broke off without finishing, and Tess could feel their two gazes winding tightly around each other. Her body was taut. Her mouth was parched, and she could not move it. They wanted each other. Even now, standing here like this. She felt it in the air.

''Just understand, it's not easy,'' he said slowly. He glanced at his watch.

''Look, I've got to be going. I was able to cancel most of my appointments this morning, but there's one particularly crusty patient I've got to see to. I have an invitation for you, though, and it might help you line up a replacement for that guest.

"There's a benefit fund raiser set for tonight put on by a group that wants to renovate an old theater. Some interesting people will be there. In fact, I think you could probably find a week's worth of guests without much effort. And I already have the tickets. Want to come?"

Tess longed to say yes, but a sense of responsibility kept her from it. She was frightened, too, by the intensity of what she'd felt just now.

"Forrest, I'd like to. But I think my place ought to be with Zach tonight."

"We could go after Zach was in bed."

She hesitated.

"Tess." He came a step toward her and took her hands in his. "When you've got a difficult interview—or maybe a particular question you want to pop to a guest on your show—how do you decide when to pop it?"

She looked at him blankly, not understanding.

"What?"

"How do you know when the time's right, Tess?"

"I—" She frowned, still trying to see what he was getting at. "When it feels right, I plunge in, that's all."

He nodded, his hands a warm cocoon around hers.

"Yes, exactly. That's what makes me go one way or another sometimes in surgery. Gut instinct telling me what's right and wrong. It's that way in any job if you're good at it. It's that way in life.

"I think that's how it was meant to be between the two of us, Tess. We're not exactly getting together under the most romantic circumstances. We haven't even known each other very long. But it feels right, Tess. Last night—I think it did to both of us. So if it feels right, let's move on it. Let's trust that gut instinct and to hell with what anybody else thinks or says."

Tess tried to absorb what he was saying, but too many things—the call from work, memories of the funeral—got in the way.

"I just don't think I'd better go with you tonight. Thank you, anyway."

"Okay," he said at last, briefly.

She could hear his disappointment.

"Forrest, I would like to continue seeing you—" She stopped. It sounded coy, and she couldn't find the right words for expressing what she wanted to say. "Unfortunately, my life is a mess at the moment. And that's not likely to change overnight."

"Sure." He forced a smile. "Well, if you should change your mind, give me a call."

Though she walked with him to the door, they didn't speak again.

Damn it, why is the timing so bad? Tess wondered. *Damn it, Forrest, why couldn't I have met you a long time ago?*

Chapter Thirteen

KATIE WAS LOOKING AT A TANGLE OF UNUSED FILM IN her editing cubicle when Tess found her. The studio around them was quieter on a Saturday afternoon than the rest of the week.

"Look at that," Katie mourned. "Two hundred feet of brilliant camera work and we're only using thirty-six of them—one lousy minute!"

"Geniuses are always underappreciated. How would you like to come with me and shoot another few hundred feet of a lady who does tole painting? Since you're here."

"The thought of it makes me want to toss my cookies, if you want the truth."

"Me, too, but I thought I'd better serve up something sweet and light."

Katie swiveled around in her chair.

"So what are you doing here? How was the funeral?"

"Over—thank God."

"P. T. find you?"

"Yes. That's why I came in." Tess shoved her hands into the deep pockets of the skirt she'd changed into for work. "It seems I've lost my guest for Monday. I hate to sound persecuted, but I think I detect the finger of my ex-mother-in-law in it. They're social acquaintances."

"Um. Well, for you I'll do tole painting. Provided you tell me about that fellow we met last night while we're on the way. Leroy and I both thought he looked to be a perfect doll.''

While she waited for Katie to ready her camera, Tess returned to her desk and made some notations on her calendar. She was straightening when Heather, entering in blue jeans, spotted her and came forward at once with hands outstretched.

"Oh, Tess, I'm so sorry!'' she said.

Tess, amused by the dramatics, lifted an eyebrow. "Oh? What about?''

Heather leaned against one corner of Tess's desk, her tight jeans accentuating the lean legs men admired.

"Since you've been so tied up, the assignment desk asked me to do a few extra features. I did one for tonight's news on Mrs. McConnaughey and that group she's starting. I had no idea you'd scheduled her to be on 'Tess and Guests' Tuesday till Earle came in and saw it on the schedule. It's too late now. I feel just terrible.''

Tess felt herself starting to redden and fought against it. *I'll bet you do,* she thought, regarding Heather, who smiled at her sweetly. *I'll just bet you and Josh cooked this up.*

"Well. That is unfortunate,'' she said, keeping her voice calm.

Two guests down, one for God knew what reason and one because of intraoffice conniving. She was fighting for her life now. She watched Heather walk away with a pert, lean swagger, then picked up the phone and opened the phone book.

"Forrest?'' she said when a voice answered. "This is Tess.''

Later, sharing a supper of grilled-cheese sandwiches and tomato soup with Zach, Tess had second thoughts about having called and agreed to go to the party Forrest had mentioned that morning. She was also more despairing than she chose to admit over events at work. Most of all, she was worried how Zach might feel about this abandonment.

"You're sure you don't mind me going out?'' she asked, not for the first time.

He glanced at her over his half-finished sandwich and shook his head. The telephone rang. He trudged to answer it and reappeared after a moment, picking up his sandwich without comment.

"Who was it?" Tess asked, folding her napkin.

"Liz Elliot. She wanted to know if I could ride bikes tomorrow. I said no."

"Zachary, why?" Tess felt exasperated. The first hint that another child was offering friendship to Zach, and he was ignoring it. Once she would have wondered if it was sexism rearing its youthful head. Now she didn't know what she should think.

"Don't want to," he said, and slid from his chair. "May I be excused?"

He went into the living room, and Tess saw him lean his forehead against the hermit crab's tank, pecking sadly, hopefully at the glass. After a moment, he became aware of her watching him, and hunching his shoulders over, walked toward his bedroom.

Go on with a normal life. Set an example, she told herself. *Don't expect too much too soon.*

She was not in a mood even to think about dressing, and as she showered, she realized she had not asked Forrest what people would be wearing tonight. Wrapped in a towel, she stood before her closet, contemplating. At last, she chose a soft-blue moiré dress wrapped at the center. As she fastened her only good jewelry, a choker of pearls, at her neck, she noticed there were deep shadows under her eyes.

Whitmore arrived, and though Zach showed little interest in it, started a Monopoly game. Forrest came to get her soon afterward. With a last tug of uncertainty, Tess said good night.

The fund-raising benefit was at the more elegant of the city's two country clubs, and shortly after they arrived, Tess found herself thinking that Forrest was like a child showing off a new toy. He dragged her about the room, his large hand engulfing hers, and every time he introduced her, he gave it a small squeeze. For the first time in days, the people around her were unreservedly kind, though from the understanding that dawned in some of their eyes as Forrest gave her name and told where she worked, it was clear some of them associated her with Zach's tragedy.

"You must be a great favorite. Everyone greets me with such warmth," she whispered.

He smiled down at her.

"Don't you know you're enough to melt an iceberg? Especially in that dress. You've got a sense of humor, but you're also smart and brave and unpretentious, and it all shows."

Tess laughed, slightly embarrassed by the fervor of his voice.

"Well, they're very nice people."

"And you haven't come across anyone you know yet?"

She shook her head.

"I guess between my job and Zach I haven't gotten out very much. And before that, with Bill, well, the people we saw were usually people he knew from work."

And they didn't have the involvement in the community or the interest in the arts, yes, even the solid financial footing that these do, she added silently. It was odd, but she felt more comfortable with this group of strangers than she had with Bill's friends. No one here seemed set on proving anything about themselves.

"Want to call and see how Zach's doing?" Forrest asked as she glanced at her watch.

"Yes, please," she said, surprised that he had read her thoughts. Not that she'd been thinking of calling; she'd merely been wondering if Zach was asleep yet. Uneasy about the use of sleeping pills, she'd avoided them for both herself and her son since Wednesday, but last night Zach had awakened in the small hours of the morning and wandered in, hunting her. Anxiety about the funeral, on top of the burger he'd had with Katie and Leroy, no doubt.

When she called, Whitmore assured her all was quiet.

"Come on," said Forrest, taking her hand again. "I want you to meet Mimi Webster."

The woman was one of the prettiest, most frivolous looking and acting platinum blondes Tess had ever met. Yet when Forrest mentioned that Mimi was deeply involved with a language tutoring program for Cambodian refugee families, the toylike façade fell swiftly away. She set Tess's mind awhirl with her understanding of language and cultural-readjustment problems.

"I'd love to be your guest on Tuesday," she said with level-eyed firmness when Tess extended an invitation. "The whole community needs to know more about the latest additions to our nation's melting pot. And merciless scrounger that I am, this may get us more volunteers."

Tess was sorry when the arrival of others disrupted their conversation. She liked Mimi Webster, was fascinated by the two sides to her.

"She's amazing," she said to Forrest.

He chuckled. "Yes, once you get beneath the eye shadow, she's all brain."

A retired judge had promised to discuss the problems of teenage runaways on her program Monday. A painter whose work was currently on display at the local art center had agreed enthusiastically to bring another painter along and debate the pros and cons of investing in original art at some future time. Tess mentally acknowledged her good fortune.

"I'm afraid you've exploited your connections with people pretty shamelessly on my account," she said. "Thank you."

Forrest stopped and looked at her seriously. "That's dumb, Tess. The people who've agreed to go on your show are exploiting you, if anything. And they'd have jumped at the chance wherever and however they happened to meet you. I happen to know some people who're doing interesting things, that's all. Now what do you say we dance?"

A five-piece combo in red jackets was playing at one

end of the room in front of a polished dance floor. Forrest held her lightly as they turned in time to the music.

"Al called before I left this evening," he said. "He asked about you."

She smiled. "He's a sweet man. It seems unusual for brothers to stay in touch the way the two of you seem to. You must have come from a very close family."

His hand stiffened almost imperceptibly on her waist.

"Not especially. Our parents were good people, I guess, but they had odd ideas concerning discipline." His eyes had hardened. "That's why Al stutters—I'd put money on it. He was scared of the dark, so for punishment they used to put him in the closet and lock the door." As though afraid he'd sounded maudlin, he smiled, tight lines surrounding his eyes. "Me, I was always too big to fit."

Underneath the joking, Tess saw a picture darker than the one he was painting, saw two little boys sheltering each other from a hostile world.

"I think you're a wonderful size," she said, touched again by his gentleness and his humility. Reaching up, she brushed her fingers briefly against his cheek. Forrest turned his head and touched his lips to them.

They melted into each other. Tess rested her head on his chest and spoke no more. The entire set the band was playing ended before her mind returned to her surroundings. She saw Mimi Webster smiling at her from a spot near the dance floor.

As Forrest led her toward a group of tables, a face nearby seemed to leap at her.

"Well, Teresa!" said a voice. It was Lucille.

Ripped from the sense of security she had been swaddled in just seconds earlier, Tess only blinked at her. Her former mother-in-law was clearly livid. Two spots of color stood out on her cheeks.

"I must say I'm surprised to see you at a gathering like this the day of a funeral," she said crisply. "Bill's going to take it rather hard realizing his son's home alone."

Tess, recovering her balance, stared past her at Bill,

who stood laughing with Caroline, oblivious. They must have just now arrived.

"Zach's with a close friend," she said, with more steel than she'd ever shown Bill's mother before. "As far as funerals go, Bill's not exactly in mourning, is he?"

She swept past so quickly Forrest caught her arm.

"Let's have a drink," he said beneath his breath. "You can wait in the hall if you want. It's more private there. Then, if you want to leave, we will."

"No. I'm mad. And there's no reason why you should have your evening spoiled."

He studied her face for a moment.

"Wait in the hall," he repeated. Then he left.

Slipping into the hallway, Tess allowed herself a moment of awe at the way she had sparked at Lucille Bondurant. But she was tired of being pushed around, tired of being criticized by the woman. She had every right to be out with Forrest tonight if she chose.

"Tess." The familiar voice intruded on her thoughts, and she looked up warily. Here came Bill.

He glanced over his shoulder as though he found the mere thought of anyone seeing them talking together distasteful.

"Just what the hell do you think you're doing here?" he demanded.

Tess gave him a long look.

"The same thing you're doing here, I'd say."

"My mother is fit to be tied!"

"Why? Because she's afraid some of her society friends might meet me and discover I don't wipe my nose on my shirt-sleeve the way she no doubt told them?"

"Don't you have any taste? Christ, dancing and living it up right after Zach—right after that funeral! People will talk."

"I doubt it. Most of those people in there seem to be pretty nice. I think what's really eating you is that after all these years the shoe's finally on the other foot. I'm having fun. I'm out with someone else, and you can't stand it.

Well, that's too bad! Now excuse me. I want to powder my nose."

Instead, she was jerked back so viciously that her teeth clicked. Bill's fingers bruised her arms as she tried to twist free of his grasp.

"I'm warning you, Tess," he said in a low voice. "You keep carrying on in public with that dentist and I'll have Zach. Judges have been known to change their views on custody, you know. In view of all that's happened, I think the chances are good."

Something snapped in Tess. Bill had never been remotely interested in having the day-to-day responsibility of their son.

"I doubt it, Bill. You've never gone after anything when the going got tough in your life!"

Slowly, his face went white. He twisted her arm around so roughly Tess swallowed a whimper.

"You smug little idiot, I'll make you eat those words! Just because you've met some guy who's out for an easy lay—just because—"

"Get your hand off her."

Forrest's voice cracked down the hall like the first warning of a volcano about to erupt. He set the drinks in his hands on a nearby table and started forward.

Bill dropped Tess's arm and swung to face Forrest. His stance was belligerent, and his eyes swiftly measured the other man's size.

"Don't try it," Forrest advised, his voice deadly quiet.

After a long moment's hesitation, Tess saw Bill's shoulders relax.

Things happened quickly then. Caroline, in an off-the-shoulder, black crepe dress, her lips polished to a shine, had entered the hallway in time to see the end of the scene. She came forward to link her fingers with Bill's. Forrest turned his arm out in a gesture, and Tess moved closer to him. Now that the worst of the clash was over, she felt weak.

"Come on, sweetheart," urged Caroline in a stage whisper, tugging at Bill. "There's no sense letting her upset you every time you see her."

Reluctantly, Bill turned away, but at the door he glanced back once.

"I'm warning you, Tess."

When they were alone, Forrest squeezed her shoulder.

"Come on. I think it's time we called it an evening, don't you?"

He did not speak again until he had let Tess into the car and slid beneath the steering wheel. Then he looked across the seat at her.

"Are you okay?"

She nodded, feeling the tightness of her own lips.

"I'm sorry," she said. "That was pretty nasty."

Forrest's face relaxed a bit. There was just a glimmer of humor.

"I don't believe your former husband likes the idea of someone else moving in on what he still looks on as his."

In the darkness, Tess felt herself blushing.

"That's pretty silly. Why, the amount of time Bill spends with Zach—"

"I didn't mean Zach. I meant you."

She had known it, but the thought made her nervous.

"That's even more absurd."

"Is it?" Forrest reached across the seat, placing his fingers lightly over hers. "The man must have had rocks in his head to let you go, Tess. It's not surprising he'd have second thoughts. From what I've seen of him, I'd say he's a jerk and deserves every one of them. The question is, do you have any?"

Tess moistened her lips before she answered.

"No. I don't have a one."

Forrest started the car and began to talk lightly about some of the people they'd met that evening. He set course for her house without even questioning if she'd like to stop anywhere else. At the front door, he kissed her briefly.

"Why don't you see if Mrs. Whitmore's free to stay

with Zach tomorrow night? I could pick you up after he's in bed for a late movie.''

Tess hesitated, wanting to.

''Oh, Forrest, I just don't think I can. I left him tonight. If anything, I should be spending extra time with him now when he needs me.''

For once, Forrest's patience sounded strained.

''You're going to be with him all day.''

''I know. But I wouldn't feel right.''

''Damn it, Tess, things don't always happen when the time's convenient. You don't have to be perfect. You don't have to be a mother all the time. Don't you realize that?''

His words struck her as harsh. She hadn't thought he would be like this.

''No. No, I don't.'' She fumbled for the doorknob. ''Good night.''

Chapter Fourteen

WHEN SHE CAME TO THE OP-ED PAGE OF THE Sunday paper, Tess groaned. There they were in black and white, three letters blasting her. From the Home and Hearth ladies? Their tone suggested it. With a crack, she folded the paper and tossed it aside. She had thought this would start to pass by now, but it seemed to be growing. *Please don't let it get any worse than it already is,* she pleaded silently.

She considered church this morning but with a shudder decided she couldn't face that. Closing her eyes, she held each side of her coffee mug and pressed her forehead against its warmth. Had it only been a week ago their world came apart?

Zach sat across from her, looking void of energy. Once he had chattered; once he had brimmed with plans. Now he said nothing, merely stared with unfocused eyes into space.

Feeling almost brutal in doing it, Tess roused him to action, insisting that he dress so they could both go for a walk in the park. If she had to prod him, she would, she told herself; she loved him. If she had to be heavy-handed in order to draw him out and into the world again, she would.

They walked, with her attempting conversation and him replying, when there was no avoiding it, with single words. When they returned, at midday, the phone was ringing.

For a moment, Tess could hardly bring herself to answer it. The day of the week, the setting, even the fair weather, was too ominously linked to seven days ago.

Gulping in air, she caught the receiver up gingerly.

"Hi. It's me," said Forrest's voice.

She sagged, relieved, though now a new premonition of unpleasantness stirred in her.

"Just thought I'd reissue my invitation to that movie," he said.

When she did not answer, he spoke again. Though his words were more measured now, they sparked the same resistance in her as those he'd spoken last night.

"Listen, Tess. You have a right to a life of your own. Apart from Zach."

Blindly, she shook her head.

"I told you, Forrest. I can't go with you. It wouldn't be right."

A long pause followed.

"All right." His words were clipped. "I don't suppose you could give me the number of that Heath girl I see on in the mornings? The one with great legs? Or maybe I should ask first, Is she single?"

"Yes. Very." Tess slammed down the phone.

Zach had not gone into his room but was lingering, watching her with interest.

"Is Forrest coming over?"

She shook her head. Had Forrest's interest in her really been that casual? Would he really turn right around and call Heather Heath?

"He wanted me to go to a movie with him tonight, but I told him I'd rather be with you. Besides," she added, needing for some reason she couldn't understand to share the fact of it with someone, "I'm mad at him."

Zach squinted at her. She thought the look was accusing.

"You're sure seeing a lot of him," he said.

"Oh, Zach, I'm not really. It's just that it's all been these last few days—" She stopped, wondering why she felt this need to explain herself and why all at once she felt vaguely angry at Zach.

"Hey, I know what we need to do," she said, turning toward the bedrooms. "Let's get into old clothes and stain the picnic table. It's going to be time to use it soon."

Zach moved to obey, but listlessly. Damn it, at least with Forrest there weren't these endless silences, Tess thought.

She wore her oldest shirt, blue plaid with a brown smudge set indelibly on one elbow from a previous treatment of the picnic table. Her jeans, faded to the color of the shirt, were rolled at the cuffs. There was something comforting about the feeling of old clothes, Tess reflected. Zach seemed more comfortable, too, plying his brush with at least a marginal interest.

Yet as the afternoon wore on, that interest lagged, and with increasing frequency Tess caught him staring into space. It had been a mistake spending today here in this neighborhood where It had happened, she thought.

This time, Zach's gaze had been fixed on the distance for some moments. Tess started to speak, then saw the look of wistfulness on his face. At the same moment, she heard the sounds he must be listening to. They were the sounds of laughter, of his friends playing.

Could she encourage him to go and join them, knowing he might be rejected? As she tried to decide, an unkempt dog with hair flopping over its eyes and tongue lolling out trotted into the yard. It belonged to a house up the street, but it came to Zach and licked him joyously. Zach very carefully wiped his hands and caressed the untidy fur.

"At least old Mopsy doesn't hate me," he muttered, burying his face against the animal.

Tess tried to speak, but the words stuck in her throat. By the time she regained control, footsteps sounded coming through the empty garage from the front of the house. An instant later, Forrest, wearing brown denim jeans and a turtleneck sweater, stepped through the door.

The last thing she needed right now was a scene. Tess rose with a hard look and started toward him.

"Hi. Heard your voices and came on through," he said. "That time of year for painting, huh?"

Tess ignored the question. "Do you make it a habit of showing up places uninvited? If you've come for Heather's number, I'm afraid you'll have to try the station."

His eyes passed easily over her.

"Leggy brunettes aren't really for me, though I've been known to make threats when pushed to the limit. Been known to try pretty damn hard to get what I wanted, too—invited or not.

"Hello, Zach. Have you finished the moldy blue ice cream yet?"

Zach had looked up from Mopsy at Forrest's entrance.

"No," he said.

Perfectly at ease, Forrest crossed to the boy and the dog and stooped to scratch the latter's ears.

"I didn't know you had a dog," he said.

Zach sat back on his heels. "I don't. I want one more than anything, but Mom says the house is too little and they're too hard to housebreak." He gave Tess a dark look that hurt.

"Oh, yeah?" said Forrest. "Well, moms have to think about those things. I live on kind of a farm, and I've been thinking of getting a dog. What kind do you recommend?"

"An English sheep dog," said Zach without hesitation. "They're kind of like Mopsy here, only big."

"I see." Forrest stood and dusted his pants. Then he fixed Zach with a quick and riveting look. "Tell me, Zach, which do you like better, steak or big juicy hamburgers cooked outdoors?"

Zach's lower jaw dropped slightly. Tess saw him swallow to keep from drooling.

"Burgers," he said.

"Well, I have both things at my house. I wondered if you and your mom would like to drive out and have a picnic."

"I guess so." Her son looked at her. "If you want."

"Go get clean clothes on, then. I'll put up the stain."

119

She turned away, silent tears sliding down her face. Because Forrest was so kind to Zach? Because he was so persistent? It wasn't safe to rely on another human being as it would be only too easy to depend on him.

She felt Forrest's hand on her shoulder.

"It's okay," he said gently. Then his attention moved back to her son. "You don't really want to change clothes, do you, Zach? Besides, I think I read somewhere that wears out your skin."

Though Zach was silent the entire trip to Forrest's house, Tess thought she detected interest in his eyes as he looked out the window. When they turned into a gravel driveway and stopped beneath an apple tree, he got out slowly.

"Boy, Forrest, you've got a big house," he said.

As they went in, with a sideways look at her, Forrest pointed out a tank that held a hermit crab. Zach pecked on the glass, then wandered on to explore the rest of the house.

"If you get hungry before I get the grill fired up, we've got cookies," said Forrest, setting down a tin from a kitchen shelf.

Zach bit into one and spoke with his mouth stuffed, and Tess was so relieved to hear him speaking at all that she didn't scold.

"How come she mostly gives me apples for between-meal snacks and you're a dentist but you give me cookies?" he asked.

Forrest bent and spoke in a tone of confidentiality. "Promise not to tell? It's how I drum up business."

They wandered around the back yard. Then Forrest brought out a frisbee, which he grew tired of tossing back and forth long before Zach did. At last Forrest announced it was time to start the grill. He had barely gotten the charcoal started when a boy of about Zach's size with ruddy red cheeks wandered out of the woods.

"Hi, Forrest," he called in greeting as he came near. "You gonna cook outside?"

Forrest looked up with a grin. "Sure am, Billy, and if

you want to join us and your folks say it's okay, I expect Zach would enjoy the company.''

The boy named Billy looked Zach up and down with open friendliness.

''I've got new calves at my house,'' he said. ''Want to see 'em?''

Zach was withdrawing, hanging back. He sent Tess a panicked look. She didn't know what was right or wrong for him, but she sensed the need to make a decision.

''Run on,'' she said gently.

After a second's hesitation, Zach fell into step with the outgoing Billy. Tess sank back in a lawn chaise and realized she was trembling.

''They'll be okay,'' Forrest reassured her. ''Billy chatters so much that Zach won't have to say a word. Why don't you just relax there and I'll bring us out a bottle of wine.''

Tess stretched out in her chair and looked about the flagstone terrace. It was such a peaceful place. And when had she last been aware of the voices of birds in trees?

''This afternoon is—like a refuge. Thank you,'' she said simply as Forrest reappeared.

He held a bottle of uncorked Burgundy. Filling a glass, he held it down to her before he spoke.

''Ah, well. I should have had the sense to think of it in the first place.'' He pulled another chaise up beside hers, facing her, and took her hand. ''I guess I was just too greedy for your company.''

Tess didn't want to meet his eyes, and so she looked down quickly, sipping her wine. They sat there together, and to her way of thinking, even the silence felt good.

''Do you entertain out here a lot?'' she asked at last.

He chuckled. ''Yeah, I entertain Billy. He can smell the grill start the minute I light the match.''

She didn't know why, but the statement warmed her. It made her believe nice things about the man beside her.

''You know, you're amazing,'' she said. ''You're—so warm and easygoing. It isn't what I would expect from someone who grew up in a family where a child was punished as cruelly as Albert was—where you must have been, too.''

"Oh, sure. I got the tar whaled out of me, especially when I got big enough to spring Albert from the closet. But by the time I was fourteen or so, I outweighed our father. They pretty much eased off us then.''

He made a joke of it, but now it was his eyes that did the avoiding. Tess swallowed, wondering what unhappiness he had known and thinking again what a kind man he was.

"I expect life's just about what we make of it,'' he said. She nodded.

"Probably not the best time to lay that philosophy on you, though, is it, after those letters this morning? Feeling some of the pressure off now that you've got guests lined up for your show?''

Tess sighed and took a long drink of wine. "Yes, thank you. But—''

She had told him about the relatively small matter of the guests she had lost; it was one reason he had helped her at the party last night. Now, on the flagstone terrace that was already growing cool enough they had drawn on sweaters, she told him the entire story of Earle's prejudice against women with children, of Heather's ambition, and of the very real jeopardy in which she saw her job.

"And Bill and his mother are pressuring me to move,'' she finished with an unhappy laugh. She did not tell him about Bill's threats to take Zach from her.

Forrest's face was a study in somberness. He still held her hand.

"And if they do let you go at the station,'' he said, looking gravely into her eyes, "what will you do?''

They were interrupted by the reappearance of Zach and Billy before she could answer. As the boys approached, Tess could see a welcome wash of pink on Zach's pale cheeks.

"Besides having a nose that picks up charcoal at two

miles distant, Billy has an excellent sense of time," said Forrest, rising. He appeared both amused and mystified by the observation. "Come on, boys, help carry the meat out. The coals are ready. Tess promised to make a salad, as I recall."

The meal came together with lazy smoothness, and while Tess and Forrest confined themselves to steak and salad, the two boys stuffed themselves with hamburgers accompanied by potato chips and followed by an excellent melon. As they ate, Tess noticed Billy observing her and Forrest with curiosity. She wondered what he'd been told about the relationship or what he imagined.

A chill moved in, reminding them it was not yet summer. They went inside for coffee, Billy vanished, and the next Tess noticed, Zach was nodding sleepily in the corner of a couch.

"Heavens, I'd better get him home," she said. She was sure he dozed the better part of the way.

When they reached her house, Zach didn't rouse when she spoke his name.

"Let him sleep," said Forrest after a second's odd hesitation. "We'll do it this way." Once more, he paused, as though unsure of the situation. Then he scooped Zach up.

But halfway up the walk, Zach started to stir. Forrest set him down with a hardness that alarmed Tess.

"There. You can walk the rest of the way. You're up to it," he said brusquely.

"I know I am!" roared Zach with unexpected anger. "What'd you carry me for? I'm not a baby."

Tess didn't know which of them she was more amazed at. Had Forrest picked Zach up just to impress her, or was his subsequent stiffness just because he wasn't used to dealing with children?

Five minutes later, she was tucking the covers over her son, who looked as though he would have a good night's sleep.

"Hey, fella, why did you get so angry with Forrest for carrying you?" she asked, kissing his cheek.

Already Zach was half oblivious, but he scowled sleepily.

"He didn't have any right to," he said in a sullen tone. "He's not my dad."

Maybe not, thought Tess as she watched his eyes close. *But I'll tell you, young man, he's done a lot today for both of us.*

Turning out the light, she returned to the living room where Forrest sat on the couch. He looked at her in invitation. She joined him. Without the need of words, he put his arms around her, and they kissed.

His kiss reached the deepest parts of her, and she returned it.

"Thanks for this afternoon," she said when at last they drew apart from one another. "It was wonderful."

"For me, too."

He kissed her again, and Tess could feel them straining toward each other. All awareness of her surroundings started to blur. She liked these sensations. She liked realizing she was a woman again. She wanted to continue forever in this intensely physical moment.

"Tess." Forrest sat back, looking at her directly, her face still tightly held between his hands. "Would your Mrs. Whitmore be willing to come over this late, do you think? It would give us a few hours by ourselves, Tess. We could go back to my place—smooth things out from where we left them the other night."

She knew what he was asking. Her hands gripped his wrists. This might be no more than one body reaching for another. But it felt like more, a great deal more.

Even if it wasn't, what did it matter? She was human. She had needs. As Forrest had said on the phone this morning, she had a right to a life of her own. And that didn't make her any less of a mother to Zach.

"All right. I'll call her and ask," she whispered.

She wouldn't worry about the future—just for tonight.

Chapter Fifteen

A COLLECTION OF FACETED CANDLE HOLDERS THREW dancing light on rock and greenery. The soothing waters of the Jacuzzi swirled across her. Tess could scarcely believe this was the same house she had left little more than an hour ago. The absence of Zach and Billy—and being in this exotic room—made it all seem different.

"Here we go, more of the wine we had at dinner." Forrest brought in a tray and set it within easy reach at the edge of the pool.

He had changed into swim trunks, and Tess looked away, too shy to let her gaze linger. But she had seen the firmness of his body and its strongly drawn masculinity. He remained there, poised above the water, until she looked up.

"Comfortable?" he asked.

But the question asked more. It asked, Are you nervous? Are you finding this awkward?

Tess nodded.

He rested a hand on her shoulder, admiring the bareness revealed by the strap of her yellow bathing suit. Tess brought her hand up and wound her fingers tightly through his. Coming here had been a pact. A promise. She couldn't back out.

Nor did she want to, except this present moment seemed so difficult. Why had everything felt so easy when she had all but given herself to him on the couch that other time?

Why couldn't she feel as natural as she had in his arms at her place just a short time ago? With suddenly rising panic, she wondered whether she was going to be unable to carry through with this.

Forrest slid into the water, sitting on the bench beside her, not too close. They sipped wine in silence; then he set his aside and with his index finger traced the corner of her mouth and up across her cheekbone.

"I hope some day I see you look less sad, Tess."

His voice reverberated, full and resonant, from rock and water. Tess smiled.

"I've been happy today."

The truth of her own words seemed to impress themselves into her mind. Maybe life was an odd mixture—far odder than she'd realized—of happy moments in the midst of tragedy and tragedy thrust into happiness. Maybe the secret was to snatch the happiness where you could.

Forrest was tracing her palm now, over and over. "I wouldn't have guessed a yellow bathing suit," he said. "Think I'd like you better in blue to match your eyes." He grinned, holding her gaze with his. "Think I'd like you without one even better than that."

The teasing comment stirred her. Tess laughed breathlessly, aware of the magnificent solidness of his chest. She reached shyly out to touch him.

Everything moved easily then. He drew her toward him, and their mouths met, open and hungry. The edge of a tooth dug into her lip once in their mutual eagerness. His tongue was incredibly soft as it curled around hers. *Why did I think this was going to be difficult?* Tess wondered. Then she ceased to think at all.

Forrest's hands were so gentle as they explored her. She felt herself swell and her senses explode at his touch. He kissed her neck, the soft skin just above her confining suit. Aroused to the limit, she felt waves of pleasure shake her. By the time they subsided, he was stripping down her suit, and they began at once to build again.

He discarded his trunks now, the water around them

intensifying the feel of bare skin against bare skin. He found her lips again, but Tess could not wait, wanting the release from this torture that only completion could bring. Forrest seemed to be reaching his limit, too. He released her mouth, and his words were labored.

"Tess—do you use anything?"

"What?" she asked, hearing as though through a haze. "Oh. No."

"Then I will." He started to move.

She caught him back fiercely. "No! Not now!"

A sound, half moan, half laughter, escaped him as he complied. With his rhythm inside her, the water without, they made love.

It's like coming home, Tess thought later when her brain was finally capable of something more than physical sensations. *It's as though I'd been waiting for this—with this man—for my whole life.*

Lifting her head from Forrest's chest, she ran fingers through his curling brown hair. He stirred and looked at her as though completely bemused.

"My God, Tess," he said, and shook his head.

She didn't understand the meaning of the comment, and she laughed. That seemed so easy now. He stood up, carrying her in his arms.

"I think we'd better adjourn to the bedroom," he said. "If we stay here much longer, we're likely to become a couple of prunes."

Like the other rooms of the house, it was large, illuminated only by the light filtering in from the hall, so that Tess could make out little more than dim shapes. The bed was low and appeared to be of Scandinavian design. Placing her in the middle of it, Forrest paused to pick up a nearby clock radio.

"There. I've set the alarm for half past twelve," he said. "It's not much time, but it's better than nothing."

"Much better." Tess, reaching for him, smiled.

He chuckled as he rolled onto her, but that bemused note was still in his voice when he spoke.

"I think you're a witch. I think you've bewitched me with that fresh-scrubbed face of yours."

"Fresh-scrubbed!" Tess groaned, then laughed. "I don't think witches are authorized to have freckles."

"Do you have freckles? I hadn't noticed. I'd better show you to the door, then. I don't allow freckles in my female companions."

Tess wondered drowsily if there were others. Not right now, judging by the amount of time he'd been spending with her. They lay contentedly in each other's arms, and the thought flashed through her mind before she could stop it: This was nothing at all like it had been with Bill.

"Tess?"

"Hmmm?"

"Your ex show any interest in having Zach? Has there been any dispute of custody, I mean?"

The question startled her, and Tess was quiet for a moment.

"Not at first. He's made a few threats since the shooting." She couldn't bring herself to tell him those threats were linked in any way with him. She frowned now. "Why?"

"No reason." He shook his head.

Before she could grow melancholy, he kissed her deeply. They moved slowly now, and with lightening spirits, Tess wondered: *Land or water? Which is better?*

Chapter Sixteen

IN SPITE OF THE FACT SHE'D HAD ONLY A FEW HOURS' sleep, Tess awoke in her own bed next morning with the feeling she could conquer the world. When she had dressed, she folded an index card in half and drew a funny face on it. "You're my favorite loon," she wrote, and propped it up on Zach's night stand where he would see it.

For a moment, she stood smiling down at him, hugging to her the fact that yesterday at Forrest's he had acted almost like a normal boy, not quite his old bubbling self, perhaps, but not lost, either. *Maybe we've turned the corner,* she told him silently.

The drive to work seemed faster than usual. Her skin tingled, and her thoughts flew as she remembered the hours with Forrest. She had never known life could be so full. This man who had come into her life understood not only her but Zach. It kindled a hope in her that she could not extinguish. Confronted with Forrest's patience, his quiet gentleness, Tess knew she had never trusted anyone so completely.

"Say, you look like the weekend agreed with you," Katie observed when they met at the coffee urn.

Tess grinned. "Yep. It did."

Then she thought of Andy Rowe's funeral and felt guilty. How could she so selfishly enjoy the world around her when a family she knew was so bereft?

But not because of Zach any more than those other boys

129

who'd taken the gun out, her logic argued. *Not because of me*.

She frowned. Was this change she felt in herself a healthy one, or was she rationalizing? After a somber thoughtfulness, she shook her head. No, what she had sensed last night, that insight, had been a valid one. Life wasn't orderly. Joy and sadness came mixed together.

She fairly breezed through the feature she did for the eight o'clock news. Her half-hour show with the retired judge she'd recruited Saturday night went beautifully. But when she'd said good-by to him, as she started back up the stairs, she found Agnes waiting in the shadows.

The receptionist hurried forward, looking behind her furtively.

"Tess, dear, I've put through two calls to Mr. Lewis this morning. I don't like to say it, but the voice sounded like the one that kept calling when there was that talk about a picket line."

"Is it still going on? How much longer?" Tess asked crossly.

Agnes fluffed her red hair.

"And the line to advertising, well, it's been blinking all morning."

Tess sighed. "Thanks, Agnes." She watched the older woman scurry away. She wouldn't let herself be frightened by the report. She wouldn't believe anything would really come of this tempest. It had been a week. Surely the worst was past.

When she returned to her desk, however, she found it hard to concentrate. As she sat lost in thought, a voice spoke, filling the chambers of her heart with ice.

"Teresa? I assume you get a lunch hour here. I'd like to talk with you."

It was Lucille.

"What a surprise," said Tess, and realized at once she didn't sound cordial. Her former mother-in-law was wearing a stunning black dress and a pinched expression.

"Apparently, the odds of finding you at home these

days are rather slim,'' she said. "I presumed this would be the likeliest place to catch you. Are you free to go?''

Tess rose, but she knew she had no intention of going to lunch with this woman. There was fire in Lucille's eye, over Saturday night, no doubt.

"I'll have to pass on lunch, but we can talk in the Green Room if you like,'' she said, gesturing.

She would hear Lucille out, and she might just tell her a thing or two as well.

Tess closed the Green Room door behind them. This was the place reserved for greeting outsiders who were to be interviewed. Its furnishings were typical outer office—a couch, a few chairs, tables, all in Danish style. Lucille looked at them distastefully as she sat down.

Everything but gloves, thought Tess, and though they were lacking, she had the mental image of Lucille Bondurant stripping them off. She spoke before her visitor could get the first word in.

"Now listen, Lucille. I'm well aware what you think of my being seen out in public with anyone just now. How it differs from Bill shacking up with someone and dragging her around, I really don't know, but neither do I care. I try to lead a decent life. I try to be a decent mother. I think I do a pretty damn good job on both counts. If you disagree, I'm sorry, but frankly I don't care.''

Behind their round glasses, Lucille's eyes had tightened and grown quite shrewd. Now they examined Tess a long moment before relaxing.

"Obviously, you have no regard for convention. That's what Bill failed to see at the start of your marriage. However, that's not really what I came here to talk about. I came because there's something I thought you might want to know about your Dr. Diadazzio—if you're concerned with being a good mother, as you say.''

Tess's body, for no reason she could explain, felt suddenly chilly. Some ugly specter, as though hinted at by Lucille's words, crouched to breathe on her.

"Forrest's a fine man, and he's good to Zach," she said in a tight voice.

But as she spoke, she realized how very little she really knew about him.

Lucille smirked. There was no other word for it.

"I suppose you do know he was engaged to be married once."

"I—we've had no reason to discuss anything like that."

She saw the victory in the other woman's face. Her knees felt weak, and Tess sat down.

"Naturally, seeing that you're out with him so frequently, I was interested."

"Oh, naturally."

Get on with it! Tess wanted to scream. She also felt a frightened, childlike urge to kick Lucille in the shins.

"It was easy enough to find out about him," Lucille said complacently. "We have friends in common. They tell me that not long after he moved here and opened his practice, he became engaged to Dacia Freemont—a very nice girl—I know her mother. Dacia was head over heels in love with him. She'd had an unhappy marriage previously, and Forrest Diadazzio treated her like a princess.

"Then, one morning, he turned up unexpectedly at her parents' house. Oh, he'd been there before and was always the soul of charm. "Who's this?" he asked when the Freemonts introduced him to two youngsters who came running through. And when they told him the two were Dacia's children, he walked out, told poor Dacia he wasn't about to be saddled with children, and canceled the wedding."

Tess's hands were twisting against the seat of the chair in total shock.

"I don't believe you!"

Lucille shrugged. "Ask for yourself."

"Forrest isn't that kind of person—and how does it happen this Dacia hadn't told him about her children in the first place?"

"I'm sure I don't know," said Lucille mildly. "Maybe

she sensed he might behave just the way he did and couldn't face losing him.''

Tess was reeling, but she tried to regain control of herself, tried not to let this smug woman see how this was affecting her. Anyway, what difference did it make? she asked herself angrily. But after last night she knew it did matter. She had trusted Forrest. Had she misjudged him?

"Well, perhaps I've painted him too unkindly,'' Lucille acknowledged. "He did give Dacia the option of continuing with the wedding—provided she'd agree to place both children in boarding schools. But Dacia was too fond of her children to agree to that. She refused, and the wedding was off.''

Lucille stood up. "Make what you want of what I've told you. I just thought perhaps you'd like to be forewarned. And, after all, Zach is my grandson.''

She put her hand to the doorknob and let herself out.

Tess sat where she was, unable to move. A ceiling she had not even known existed seemed to crash down about her.

Have I been a complete fool? she asked herself, exhausted. She had believed in Forrest's basic goodness, certainly. She could not imagine his acting as Lucille said. Yet she found herself remembering things: facts and comments that she had, perhaps, tried to shrug off; Forrest's annoyance when she first had refused to go to the party with him; and, later, his statement that she should have a life of her own apart from Zach.

Apart from Zach! But surely he had not meant it that way. And yet . . .

And yet she did not know how he had meant it. She had questioned so little. She had been too quick to bask in the protective warmth he seemed to offer both her and Zach.

Perhaps she had almost made the same mistake, relying on Forrest, that she'd made with Bill. It was treacherous putting too much emotional trust in anyone but yourself. She'd chosen to forget that these last days; she'd lived by emotion rather than logic. Perhaps—

"Tess? You've got a phone call," said P. T., putting her head in.

Tess felt as though her desk were miles away, with snowdrifts pulling at her thighs every step of the way.

"Just me," said Forrest's steady voice. "Thought I'd see if I could pick you and Zach up for spaghetti somewhere tonight."

"I can't," she said. No excuses, no explanations. Anyway, she recalled now Zach squinting at her yesterday and saying, with disapproval, perhaps, that she'd been seeing a lot of Forrest. She remembered, too, Forrest's brusqueness when he'd put the boy down the night before.

There was a pause, and then he spoke again.

"I miss you."

Her eyes filled with tears. How had she let herself get so involved with him—with anyone—just now?

"I've got to go. 'By," she said briskly.

Guilt wrapped itself around her like a muffler. She turned to work. It was wrong to hurt Forrest, and she felt miserable, but she had all she could do surviving just now.

The rest of her work day was ghastly. Only the station's least adept cameraman was available to accompany her for one of her short features that afternoon. She came back with the leaden feeling it had not gone well.

When she walked into the corral, her phone was ringing.

"Hi, Tess," said a voice when she answered. "This is Moe-in-the-Afternoon at WPET. A lot of our listeners have been talking about you this afternoon, and I thought we ought to give you a chance to tell your side of the troubles you're having. What do you think? Do you still feel comfortable with your choice of having been a working mother in view of what's happened?"

She could hear the beep, telling her anything she said would be on the air.

"I don't have anything to say," she answered, and hung up.

Immediately, the phone was ringing again.

"Are you sure you don't want to comment, Tess? One lady just said she thinks our movement toward equality in the last ten years has been just an excuse for selfishness. She says if you were a sensitive person, you'd accept the fact people are disappointed with you and give up your show. Surely you want to make a reply to that!"

Tess closed her eyes, pressing a fist against her forehead.

"Please—just let me alone!"

How could this station do it? she wondered. But for WPET and its sloppy sensationalism, no one would have known about Zach—about her.

She opened her eyes and saw a letter laid out in the stack of new mail awaiting her perusal. *I wept when I read those angry letters to the editor about you. I work, and I have a preschooler, and sometimes I feel guilty. . . .*

There was more at stake here than her own feelings, her own job. If she didn't stand up to this small, vocal group, a lot of other women would be made to feel guilty.

The phone was ringing again—three times—four times. She could walk away. Ignore it. If she were wise, she would. Instead, she picked it up and heard Moe-in-the-Afternoon with his bright talk-master style asking once again if she didn't want to respond.

Tess's mind worked methodically, weighing what she could say that would not make this worse and that would in no way reflect on the station.

Beep.

She gathered her breath and plunged in.

"I'm a public figure. It wouldn't be ethical for me to take sides on issues. As to my personal life—my child—I've done the best I can. Isn't that all any parent can do, really? We're all different people. We see things different ways. I don't like to think that makes any of us right or any of us wrong."

She hung up even though Moe-in-the-Afternoon was speaking again. Too much? She didn't know. She'd been generous, at least, when she really believed the Home and

Hearth League or any other group that thought its way was the only way *was* wrong.

The phone calls, the hassles, Lucille . . . Today she was more than a little glad that it was quitting time.

By the time she got home and Whitmore left for the day, Tess was almost overwhelmed by the need to see Zach. He's all I've got, she thought, and she ached with the need to brush back his rumpled hair. It was wrong. Mothers who put that sort of burden on their children smothered and did terrible things to them. But now, in this immediate afternoon, she felt a sense of grief and loss and knew the sight of him would comfort her.

There seemed no point in sticking to the old patterns she had established to spare him teasing by his peers. His friends had closed him out of their lives, so she walked down the street to meet him. He was lagging behind, just passing Andy Rowe's house, which must be a torture to him. She stopped and waited.

The front door of the Rowe house opened. A white-haired woman—one of the grandmothers, Tess supposed—flew out.

"Murderer!" she screamed, leaning over the wrought-iron porch railing. "You little murderer! Get out of here!"

Tess gasped and plunged across the street without thought of traffic.

"Come on," she said, catching Zach by the hand. And she could feel that he was trembling.

The woman on the porch slammed back inside without Tess's noticing. Had she spoken again? Screamed more abuse? Tess didn't know.

"Has that happened before?" she asked in a tight voice. Zach scuffed his toe.

"She waits for me," he finally said.

The revelation filled her with a fury she couldn't conquer. The cruelty, the utter cruelty of it, she protested inwardly. She could understand it. She could appreciate the grief and resentment. However, she could not stand by and let this sort of thing be directed at Zach.

She set him down in the living room and gripped his hands tightly between her own.

"That's wrong. It's very wrong," she said. "That woman is calling you names because she's hurting inside, but it's still very wrong."

She left him there, still slightly too disoriented herself to think of distracting him, and picked up the phone. With a shaking finger, she dialed the Rowes' number.

"Annette?" she said when the voice that answered was Andy's mother's. "This is Tess Bondurant. I'm sure the last thing you want is to hear from me, but—I'm sorry—" She brushed at her eyes. "I feel I have to talk to you about—about this calling names at Zachary. If I could come over and see you just for a moment . . ."

The voice on the other end was strained but did not sound hostile.

"I think it would be better if I walked over there. Is now all right?"

"Yes."

Tess hung up and looked at her son.

"Andy's mom is coming over. Why don't you go to your room?"

He slipped away in silence.

The hermit crab, in his glass cage, climbed a tree branch. His minute sounds were audible to Tess. When the doorbell rang, she recoiled. Then, with a sense of the inevitable, she went to face Annette Rowe.

When the door opened, they looked at one another for a moment.

"I'm sorry," Tess said, and wondered whether the other mother could possibly understand what that word meant.

Annette Rowe gave a twisted smile.

"So am I," she said.

Tess gestured awkwardly. "Come in. Sit down."

Andy's mother stepped into the house but shook her head.

"I won't stay."

They had not been the sort of neighbors to visit back and forth in each other's kitchens, but they had chatted in both their yards and laughed about the things their two sons did. Now Tess knew nothing she could say would make this easier for the two of them.

"I feel so sorry—so terribly sorry about what happened to Andy. I know that's only words. It seems inadequate." Tess paused. "I know I must seem heartless complaining to you. But Zach has suffered in all this, too. He's become an outcast among his friends, and today, when he passed your house, a woman came out on the porch and called him names."

Annette nodded with a weariness beyond her years.

"Andy's grandmother. I'm afraid this has all been just too much for her. My husband is an only child, you see, and Andy was her only grandchild—" She broke off and swallowed. "I'm sorry, Tess. I heard her shouting things once before—terrible things. I told her she mustn't, but she's so upset. A little crazy, I think. They're leaving tomorrow. It won't happen again."

"Thank you." Tess drew a breath. "I'm sorry you had to come here. I should have come to you."

"It was better this way."

They went out onto the front step, and all of a sudden Tess was aware of another presence beside her. Looking down, she saw Zach. His face was pinched, and he stayed close beside her.

"I didn't mean to hurt Andy," he said to Annette Rowe.

The woman's mouth shook violently. For a moment, Tess was terrified she would collapse.

Then she extended a hand and rested it on Zach's head.

"I know," she said with effort. Turning, she walked quickly away.

Next door, Laurel, who hadn't spoken to Tess or Zach since the accident, had pulled into the driveway in time to witness the scene and was staring at them. Tess turned her son gently and nudged him inside.

"So you see," she said, looking down at him and trying to smile, "Andy's mom doesn't hate you. She understands accidents happen, just like I told you. She understands what happened wasn't your fault."

"But it was!" objected Zach, and burst into tears.

He circled her waist with his arms, as he had circled her legs just a few years back, and buried his face against her. "It *was* my fault partly. I knew I shouldn't play with a gun. You'd told me that. You'd told me kids did it sometimes and it was dangerous and what could happen. You'd told me, but I went ahead and did it, anyway. I was stupid!"

His weeping was so prolonged and so intense it frightened Tess. At last, she was able to steer him into his bedroom where he fell asleep, still wracked by sobs. *And we're back at square one,* she thought, sitting beside him. Feeling ancient and defeated, she rose and walked back into the empty living room.

Maybe Bill had been right about moving—for all the wrong reasons, she thought. Maybe it would be best for Zach to get away from here. Then, every face he saw, every yard and tree he passed, would not be a silent reminder that Andy had once been alive and now was dead.

Picking up her purse, she dug out a piece of paper. She had put it there last week, which now seemed a century ago. On it were the numbers of two stations that had advertised in a trade journal, both with job openings she might possibly fill. The stations were small. Neither offered a chance to do her own show, but that didn't matter. What mattered was finding a job that would support her and her son, even something outside television, just so long as it gave Zach the chance at change he needed.

Oklahoma or South Dakota? She stared at the numbers. Oklahoma—for God's sake, she wasn't even quite sure where that was on the map.

But then, in a different sense, I'm not really sure of my own location just now, either, she realized.

Not after what Lucille said about Forrest.

Not after the angry letters and radio shows.

Not after this.

Chapter Seventeen

BOTH STATIONS SAID THEY'D CONSIDER HER IF SHE'D send tapes. They even sounded fairly interested. She'd have to work out details with Bill, of course, since he had visitation rights. Well, a lot of good it did for all he exercised them. She'd pay Zach's way back to visit him summers and holidays. That should go a good way toward pacifying him.

Tess sat and let darkness close in without putting on lights. The ringing of the front bell startled her. With her run of luck today, she thought as she went to answer it, this would be Bill.

But it was Forrest, and his expression even on first glance was wary.

"I thought I'd stop by and see what was the matter," he said, stepping in without invitation. "You sounded pretty chilly on the phone this morning."

Tess made an aimless gesture with her hands.

"I was busy. I'm sorry."

"In that case, what about dinner?"

She turned and began to move aimlessly toward the bookcase, unable to face him.

"No."

"You're confusing me, Tess. Something must be the matter then. What is it?"

"Look, you knew my life was a shambles from the moment you met me. That's all there is to it!"

She knew she spoke more vehemently than he deserved, and she was ashamed of herself. How could she explain the terrible doubts Lucille had stirred with her story that morning? Anyway, whether that was true or not was academic now, since those phone calls. It was unimportant, and if he was flawed, she did not want to know it.

Yet she voiced the question, anyway, feeling it almost dragged from her.

"Is it true you were engaged to be married and broke it off because the woman had children?"

She heard him stir, and she glanced toward Zach's room, wondering if their voices would wake him.

"I suppose you could sum it up like that," Forrest said dryly.

Tess swung to look at him, surprised by the bluntness of his admission. Still she could not bring herself to believe there was not a deep core of goodness in him. She knew she was hurting him.

"I had no right to ask that," she said, sinking into a chair. "It just . . ." She let the thought dwindle.

He had made a difference in her life. She was not at all sure she would have come through this last week without his support, his reassurances, the Superman ice cream. Yet she knew already that things were unworkable, didn't she? And they had not even begun what could be looked on as a full-blown romance. Oh, they had been sexually intimate, but in this day and age, that was no sort of promise even though it had been— She shook her head to clear it of the memory and felt a strange mist in her eyes.

"Forrest, please don't hate me. I know I'm not handling this very well, and I think you're probably the kindest, most patient man I've ever known. You do deserve better. But the fact is—" She tried for breath, but her lungs seemed incapable of inflating. "The fact is, there's no point in going out with you tonight. It would only make things harder. Out of—of stubbornness or something, I haven't faced up to what I have to do to help Zach forget the worst of this nightmare. Today I did. We've got to move. I've applied for two jobs. Out of state. If neither comes through, I'll look for something else, but we've got to get away.''

She paused, all at once aware she had expected—hoped for, perhaps—some strong reaction. There was none, though his face was tightly set.

''I meant what I said before, Forrest. You've been—'' Her voice shook. ''You've been wonderful! You've done so much for Zach—you've tried to reach him. I want you to know I'm grateful, and I always will—''

''Grateful!'' His echo drowned her out. He took a scant step toward her, and she could see his anger. ''Well, that's damn nice of you! It happens I've had some very grateful patients, too.''

''Forrest, I didn't mean—''

''After last night—in view of last night—I'd hoped what you felt might be just a little more than gratitude. But then I've always been a fool about women, I guess.''

He turned and walked out. Tess leaned deep into the chair holding her and closed her eyes, wondering why she felt such a huge and overwhelming sense of loss. Was she in love with Forrest? Of course she was. She'd been an idiot, trying to hide that fact from herself so she wouldn't be hurt, but she couldn't deny it. Letting him touch her heart had been a misstep, one for which she now must pay.

This was for the best. She sat and let the pain wash over her.

''Mom?''

Zach looked shadowy in the distant light of the single lamp she'd turned on.

''Is somebody here? I thought I heard voices.''

He was still half asleep. Tess held out her arm, and he came and wedged himself in beside her. As she rested her cheek on his head, she thought she might burst from some strange combination of love and loneliness.

''No,'' she said, looking beyond the pool of light surrounding them toward darkness. ''No, there's no one here.''

Chapter Eighteen

IN THE PARKING LOT UNDER THE WNNB LOGO, TESS slammed on her brakes. All the way to work she had thought of changes, had tried to cheer herself with the thought that by biting the bullet yesterday and making those phone calls, she had bought herself and Zach a measure of peace. Let Earle win; let Heather have the job she coveted; let the going be hard somewhere else. At least the constant threat of turmoil would no longer hang above her head at work, she'd thought.

Now she stared in dismay at the scene before her. Bundled in jackets against the chilly morning, a long line of people wound back and forth in front of the station, blocking entrance. *Fire Tess Bondurant*, read one sign. *Let Tess Try Being a Mother!* said another. *Channel 31 Ignores Its Viewers. Get a real WOMAN for a Woman's Show*.

Men, women, and preschool children—many, many children—were walking the picket line. Above them fluttered a red, white, and blue banner reading Home and Hearth League.

Slowly, Tess stepped out of her car. She felt shock. Queasiness. Revulsion. How could this be happening now? She hadn't really believed it would happen at all.

Now she saw there were cars and cameras from other stations here. Someone spotted her and pointed in her direction. Stubbornly, with a sense of one more ordeal to face, she began to walk. To her sudden relief, she saw

144

Katie and the black technician who worked the morning shift leave the studio entrance and push through toward her.

"The things you do to boost your share of the ratings," said Katie in greeting.

Tess couldn't manage a smile. She was hypnotized by the ugliness of that line.

"How long?"

"Who knows." Katie jerked her head in angry dismissal. She linked her arm through Tess's. "Come on."

"Are you sure—" Tess looked from Katie to the technician. "Maybe you two should go on back. Let me cross on my own."

The technician grinned. "Hey, I'm an expert at this—from the other side. I made the scene in Selma before I was even dry behind the ears. These folks are your basically gutless, troublemaking types," he added, loudly enough to be heard, as they reached the ring of people. "They won't throw anything."

Tess heard sneering voices, shouts, insults. She saw a microphone come at her.

"Not to worry—Leroy and a few of the others of Springfield's finest are here to keep this all friendly," Katie said, glaring back at a stout man who reluctantly fell back and let them through.

Then the door to the station brushed open. They were safe. Tess felt herself trembling. And there, waiting just inside with hands on his hips, was Earle Lewis.

His blue eyes were cold and hard in his tanned face.

"Well, I hope you're satisfied. Once our fellow stations put this on the air, there's going to be hell to pay."

He offered no pretense of sympathy, only concern for his damned station.

"I didn't really believe it would come to this," Tess said simply.

He ignored her.

"I'll put it to you one last time, Tess. Are you going to

145

take that production assistant's job so I can go out and tell that mob out there you're off the air, or must I fire you?''

Tess's eyes smarted with the cruelty of his words. Was she satisfied? he'd asked. What had she done except not be a coward, except stand up for what she still believed in the depths of her heart was right?

"Neither one," she said, unbuttoning her coat and tossing back her hair. "You can tell them I've just given notice."

Without looking back, she stepped around him and started toward the stairs.

"Tess, wait!" Katie came running to catch up with her. "You're crazy! You don't have to do that, you know. You can fight it—take legal action, plenty of things."

Tess shook her head.

"It's no use, Katie. I'm sick of it. I can't put Zach through any more of what he's going through in that neighborhood, and I can't take any more of what I'm going through here. I've already started hunting another job. And you know what? It feels pretty good. At least now I won't have to worry about those damn phone calls!"

Giving up the attempt to keep pace with her or to reason with her, Katie fell back. Tess marched up the stairs, controlling anger in each step.

"Where's Heather?" she said to the assignment desk as she reached the corral.

The bespectacled man in charge of it looked at her sadly.

"Up in Urbana," he said. "Be back about half past ten. Sorry about that fracas out there."

Back at half past ten. Well, that left it up in the air who would do her show. P. T. could take over today, or Tess could do it and let Heather make her debut tomorrow. She banged out a note to that effect and left it on Earle's desk.

The phone was ringing when she returned.

"Tess?" It was Whitmore's voice. "Is something going on there? I just heard on the radio—"

"Yes," cut in Tess, and felt a white-hot fury that Zach

might be subjected to this, which could only confirm his belief in the damage he'd done. "And I don't want Zach to know about it, Whitmore. Do you understand? *He must not know!*"

She banged down the receiver. A cameraman sidled up to her.

"Good God, Tess, is it true you've given Earle your notice?"

"Yes," she said shortly, and turned away.

Four TV sets by Josh Jergens' desk were tuned to four other stations. It was a time when morning news breaks might flash on, and she wanted to hear for herself what was said if this was one of them. She walked over and watched the screens, ignoring Josh.

He drew twice on his curving pipe, then took it from his teeth.

"Look, Tess, I am damn sorry—"

"Shut up, Josh." She didn't even move her eyes to really look at him.

As though too startled to answer, he returned the pipe to his mouth. A second later, one of the screens in front of her flashed to a news break.

"There's trouble at Channel 31 in Springfield today, where a group of protesters are demanding the dismissal of talk-show hostess Tess Bondurant." A male reporter was shown standing just outside the door she'd entered not long ago—or it seemed like not long ago, though it had been more than an hour.

Now a woman with two small children in tow was speaking into the camera, which jumped slightly. Her voice was breathy and sweet.

"I'd never want to hurt anyone, but we have to make a stand somewhere," she was saying. "The problem with our country and our families today isn't TV violence or video games or any of the other things people try to blame. It's absentee mothers!"

For once, Tess felt no reaction other than a cynical acceptance.

"Phone call, Tess," said the reporter who sat in front of her, strolling over. "It's Arlington Hutchins. He's some sort of lawyer. I bet he's heard about the picket line and wants to represent you."

But the name clicked with Tess. It was Bill's mother's lawyer. She felt a small, cold lump of fear. Trust Lucille to hear about this first thing, she thought bitterly. Didn't anyone do anything all day but sit around watching television? What if Bill and Lucille tried to get Zach from her now, just when she'd burned all her bridges?

"Tell Mr. Hutchins I'm busy," she said grimly.

Two more calls came in quick succession, both from other media wanting a statement. Tess refused those, too.

She went into the library and began to collect demonstration tapes for her job hunting. At five before ten, Mimi Webster swept in.

"What the hell is going on out there?" she asked, shrugging out of a white fox jacket that matched her platinum curls.

"You mean the picket line's still there?" *They must be writing for a formal announcement on the noon news,* Tess thought.

"No one's really taking it seriously, are they?" asked Mimi, lighting a cigarette.

"Are, were, and would be except that I've given my notice. I'm sorry you had to wade through it all."

Mimi looked at her in surprise. "Honey, it takes more than that to intimidate me. But I'm sorry to hear you've quit. And Forrest will be crushed. He thinks you're only one step short of Barbara Walters' league, you know."

Tess smiled and drew in tightly on her emotions. She wouldn't allow herself to think about Forrest.

With Mimi chattering easily, she led the way to the Green Room. There still had been no word from Earle on who would be the hostess on "Tess and Guests" today. By ten past ten, there had been no sign of P. T., either.

"Excuse me," Tess said, interrupting the good-natured

Mimi. ''There's something I've got to check about the show today.''

She was not three steps away from Earle's office when Heather, with a swinging stride, came in from the hallway accompanied by a cameraman.

''Congratulations,'' Tess said, looking at her. ''It seems you've got yourself a show.''

This time, Heather did not make a pretense of camaraderie. A smile of complete satisfaction stole over her face.

Tess knocked twice on Earle's door, then opened it without waiting.

''Heather's back, and I haven't had a reply from the note I left you,'' she said in a cool voice. ''Who are you counting on to take the show today?''

He leaned back, appraising her as though taking note of this audacity. His gaze traveled on through the open door to Heather. Her hair was wind-blown, her cheeks whipped with color, and judging by the heaving of her chest, she'd run up the stairs.

''She's out of breath,'' said Earle with obvious irritation. ''Has she had the background on this morning's guest?''

''No.''

''You go on, then. It makes more sense than throwing that excitable assistant on for just one day. Show Heather the ropes, though. She may be able to pick up something, though she didn't seem to have much trouble the day she filled in. Tomorrow you go through the prep time with her and be on the sidelines.''

''I hadn't really expected to come in tomorrow,'' Tess said stiffly.

He gave her a long, hard look.

''That's not a very professional attitude, Tess.''

She wondered why that should matter to him in the least now.

''Screw professional attitude. All right. I'll be here.''

She ducked out again. ''Heather—Earle wants you to

come with me now. He thinks you should have this one last chance to ask questions before you go off on your own tomorrow.''

"I don't have any questions," said Heather, obviously annoyed, as she broke off conversation with two male coworkers.

"Probably not. But that's what Earle wants."

Tess continued toward the Green Room, and after a moment, Heather followed.

It was time now to take Mimi Webster downstairs to the studio. She had made that incredible switch of gears and was throwing out hard, intelligent facts about the adjustment problems of refugee families. Heather was undisguisedly bored. Tess wondered whether she was even listening to the conversation.

On the yellow couch in front of the fake kitchen, Mimi adjusted herself as Jack, with his white card, checked the lighting and made a few wisecracks.

"I think I know well enough what goes on from here," said Heather, all but yawning. "I'll watch from the sidelines. And starting tomorrow, Jack, we can drop this silly business with the card."

Jack dropped the card to his side and spoke through bared teeth.

"Listen, you conceited little broad, if I'm going to have to work with you, you'll damn well park your butt six inches from wherever mine is today and try to watch things with my eyes. It's that kind of teamwork that makes a show go—which Tess well knows. If you think you're too good for that, I'm warning you, toots, I won't lift a pinkie to help you out if something goes wrong."

From the neck up, Heather was crimson.

"You stupid—I'll report you for this!"

"Report," said Jack laconically. "One minute, Tess."

Mimi Webster was suppressing laughter. With a vengeful look at him, Heather moved to Jack's side. The lights were already on, the finger signals were starting, and Tess felt a strange sense of release. There would be no more tension as the time for phone calls neared, no more worries about lost ad accounts. When Jack's finger went down, it would be her last time on this set.

"Hello. Good Tuesday morning," she said.

And suddenly it hurt to know she'd never say those words again.

Chapter Nineteen

TESS GAVE HER SON NO CHOICE IN THE MATTER OF SUP-
per. She simply announced that night that they were
going out. Away from the phone, away from the TV and
its announcement of her resignation "for personal reasons" on the evening news. Away from everything and
everyone. Unreachable.

They pulled into the parking lot of a pizza place that
Zach had always liked.

"I don't want to go in," he said. "I'll wait in the car."

"Why ever not?" Tess asked severely. She knew it was
sounding too hard on him, but her patience was worn thin.

"We might see somebody who knows us—and people
look at me funny."

"You didn't worry about that the night we went out
with Forrest," she argued, taxed to the limit.

Zach shrugged. "That was different."

"All right. We'll go someplace farther from home,"
Tess said. "But you *will* go in."

When she stopped at a second pizza house, he dragged
in meekly. But when Tess asked if he wanted a soft drink
before their food came, he shook his head.

"There was trouble today at the station, wasn't there?" he
said as they waited for a large deluxe with no anchovies.
"I heard Laurel come over from next door and ask Whitmore
about it when I was leaving for school."

"That hypocrite!" The accusation burst from Tess. "How

dare she come to our house and—and pry when she hasn't even had the decency to speak—when she's *ignored* us ever since—''

She didn't finish. Zach looked at her with sad, solemn eyes.

If only I knew what you needed, she thought. *If only I knew how I could reach out and heal you.*

''What did Laurel and Whitmore say?'' she asked, curious how much he knew.

''I dunno. Just that there was trouble at the station and that it had something to do with you.''

Tess took a breath. Might as well blunder through it.

''Yes, there was trouble,'' she said. ''There were people there carrying signs, people who didn't think I ought to be allowed to keep my job.''

''Because of me?''

''No! Not because of that. It was because—well—some people aren't very happy about some of the things I've said on my show. And I don't like working there if things are going to be like that. So I told them today I was quitting to look for another job.''

She held her breath, expecting him to ask where that other job might be, but mercifully he didn't. That sort of thing didn't occur to a child unless you mentioned moving far away, she supposed, and at the moment she was not about to do it.

''Oh,'' he said, and the pizza arrived. He toyed with a piece without eating it. ''Is Dad going to have a day with me this week?'' he asked as though that followed in logical sequence.

''I don't know,'' she said. She hadn't thought about it. Now that she did, she realized she must have taken a rather sizable mental step, all but crossing Bill out of their lives. A realist at last, she told herself. She supposed she should call Bill and badger him about an outing for Zach's sake—but no, she could deal with only so many difficult things at one time.

''Let's find something fun to do this weekend if you

don't do something with him," she said, and forced a smile.

Zach didn't answer.

That night, Tess slept poorly, unable to turn her mind off as it played and played again the scenes at work, the unhappy parting with Forrest. When she did sleep, the dreams were worse. She was there watching Zach and Andy Rowe with a gun between them, screaming for them to stop, to put it down—but her words were soundless; she was opening a closet door to find Zach in the corner, his body curled and shrunken like a mummy. At four in the morning, she woke up drenched in sweat and went into the kitchen for a glass of milk. After that, she slept soundly, awaking a few hours later feeling as though she had run a marathon.

By the time she had dressed and had coffee, the morning paper was at the door. She opened it and looked with disgust at the local news page. There in black and white was a picture of the picket line at her station. Annoyed with herself for whatever compelled her to wallow in unpleasantness, she began to read the accompanying story.

Like the news break she'd watched the morning before, the story before her featured quotes from "a mother with two small children," either seized on because she was particularly articulate or more likely because she was engagingly visual with tots in tow.

"We're just a lot of individuals who care about children and families," she'd told the reporter writing the story. "We think it's wrong for a woman whose child was off doing things he shouldn't have been to tell other people how to run their lives. If she'd been home with her child those precious years when he was growing up, this might not have happened. Something happens to children—to their minds and *feelings*—when they're left to grow up with strangers or in day-care centers. Our group knows that.

"We don't feel Tess Bondurant represents the values of the people her program is aimed at—housewives, mothers who stay home with their children. I guess values are what's most important to us. That's why we want her off the air."

There were, of course, mealymouth comments: how they felt sorry for Tess, sorry for her little boy. A light tap sounded on the kitchen door. Whitmore was here. Tess threw the paper down in a heap and headed for the station.

When she pulled into the parking lot, she was surprised to find a sizable number of pickets back in place. They stood in small clumps today, though, not in a line. She got out resolutely and walked toward them.

"See? She's back," one hissed as she passed. "I just knew they wouldn't keep their word. It's a good thing we came back!"

The viciousness in the voice made Tess shudder. Had she once dismissed this group as merely a harmless, behind-the-times bunch of comic characters? They appalled her now.

Oh, do be quiet. I'm only here to help my replacement, she wanted to say. Instead, she looked glinty-eyed at the woman who had spoken. This was Earle's problem now. She wasn't going to do or say a thing.

As she entered the studio, Agnes stood up from her desk and came toward her.

"I'm sorry," Agnes said, and her wrinkled mouth quivered. "I'm ashamed of this station for the way they've treated you."

"Thank you, Agnes. Your kindness makes it easier." Tess smiled.

But Agnes didn't hurry back to tend her phones as was her custom.

"I know it must be hard with your little boy and having to hunt another job and all," she said. "If you need a little help, well, I've got money squirreled away that I could lend you."

On impulse, Tess leaned forward and hugged her.

"I'll remember, Agnes. Truly. And thank you."

Wiping at the telltale dampness that had crept into her eyes, she went up to the control room. On the monitors, she watched the curved news desk with Matt and Ollie and Heather, now inheritor of all that once had been hers.

There was a movement from the tyrant who ran this domain and who even now was plugged into earphones, listening, observing. Without taking his eyes from the equipment he was watching, he extended an arm and thrust a piece of paper toward her.

You should sue the bastards! he'd scrawled across it.

Tess smiled at him, too, but he didn't look up.

In the corral, Tess hung up her coat and started the task of cleaning out her desk. Katie was already out on assignment. Tess felt as though all ties had already been severed.

Have I been defeated? she asked herself. *Have I been a quitter? No, slinking back to my production assistant's job would have been the easy way out. Moving will hurt, but it's also rejecting defeat.*

Methodically, she began to lay aside files on all the guests she still had scheduled. Inside were press clippings, things the people had told her, things she wanted to ask. Today's guest would be the woman whose children had been kidnapped by her ex-husband and taken out of state where the law couldn't touch him—a growing problem. Tess had given that file to Heather yesterday.

Now Tess paused and frowned in thought. She hoped Heather managed to get along well with the guest. The woman was in agony over what had happened. Heavens! Who wouldn't be? Though gritty, she was shy, would never have talked about this except to spare other mothers the trauma of "snatching," and Tess had seen she required delicate handling or she would clam up.

Well, she would mention it to Heather, who would probably be offended. Tess eyed the clock, then jumped as the phone in front of her rang.

"Mrs. Bondurant?" said an excitable voice the instant she picked it up. "This is Albert Diadazzio."

The line echoed just enough to let her know it was long distance.

"Hello, Albert," she said before realizing the informal name had slipped out.

"Mrs. Bondurant—Tess—what's happened? Why have you told Forrest you didn't want to see him?" he asked, giving her no chance to say more.

"Albert, it's rather complicated. I'm changing jobs and—and it just wouldn't have worked out." She finished quickly, for she saw Earle and another man whom she didn't know heading toward her. She was moved by Albert's concern, but this was hardly the time or place to discuss it.

"But he *cares* about you!" the voice on the phone was fairly shouting. "And if anyone deserves some happiness, it's Forrest."

"Albert, I know." She tried to soothe him. "He's—he's wonderful. But I heard about his engagement, how it came to an end because he didn't want the children around, and I have Zach and—"

She broke off, partly because she felt too vulnerable, knew she was betraying some vague thought to the future that she ought never have had, and partly because Earle and the other man now were in earshot. Earle looked displeased, she noted. But on the other end of the phone, Albert was leaping into the conversational breach.

"You think Forrest doesn't like children? You think he would mistreat them? My dear woman, I think Forrest did what he did—remaining single all these years—precisely because there's nothing more repugnant to him than the thought of hurting a child!"

She heard him gulp in just enough air for further speech and then rush onward.

"Forrest and I were abused as children. I speak dispassionately, let me assure you—from strictly a professional and a legal viewpoint. Forrest was beaten terribly. Not spanked. Beaten. Never for real misbehavior but for disobeying, which usually meant helping me out in some way. They used to lock me in—"

Tess heard the long pause, knew Albert was gathering himself, stoically refusing to stutter. She could not even glance at the two men standing beside her desk. She could not tear herself away from what she was hearing. It was horrible. More horrible than anything she had ever imagined. And she knew that in some way now she had been part of the horror.

"They used to lock me in the closet to punish me—because I was afraid of the dark, you see," Albert finished. "Forrest used to let me out. The last time, they beat him so severely that they broke his nose and chin. The hospital where they took him reported them, and after that the two of us were put in foster homes."

Tess shaded her eyes with her hand. "I didn't know," she said.

"Well, of course not." Albert sounded prickly. "Do you suppose it's the kind of thing anyone talks about? But Forrest is as aware as I am that the chances of being an abusive parent are increased by that sort of background. We've never talked about it, even between ourselves, but I've always felt that's why neither one of us has risked becoming involved—"

Interrupting himself, he sighed gustily. "The point is that until last night he's sounded so happy the last few times we've talked. I knew he was spending time with you and your son, and from what he said—well, it was clear he didn't expect it to end like this.

"Please. I know I shouldn't interfere like this, and I've lost my temper. But you're a woman of compassion; I know it from your sensitivity toward your child. Try to understand Forrest. He gives so much of himself. Be the one who gives him something back. Try to work this out, won't you, please?"

Her cheeks were wet. Tess brushed at them, not caring what Earle and the man who was with him thought.

"I don't think I can," she said with effort. "I wish I could—I'd give quite a lot if I could—but I don't think I can."

She hung up because she knew if she spent any more time with Albert, she'd break down completely. Already she was beginning to hate herself.

But why, a part of her cried desperately? *I only did what was reasonable—what was rational. Forrest and I had only known each other for a week, after all, and there were no promises made, none even hinted at. I can't base my future and, more importantly, Zach's on something nonexistent. I have to find another job; we have to move on. There really isn't any other way.*

"Yes?" she said to Earle, her lips so stiff that she could scarcely form the word.

"This is Norman Mathes from the *Dayton Daily News,*" Earle said, his tone revealing nothing. "He wanted to know if we'd object to your talking to him about the problems here and your decision to resign. Since technically you're free of us now, I felt it only fair to tell him he could talk to you if you chose."

Inasmuch as she was able to feel anything relating to this present moment, Tess registered a mild surprise at the extent of his fairness. Earle, who must know she might mention his prejudice against working mothers, who must know she could levy dark charges against this station, was nonetheless not trying to block her. Or was it simply some principle of freedom of the press he was upholding? Whichever it was, she knew it didn't matter.

"Well, I don't choose," she said, and turned back to a desk drawer in a gesture of dismissal.

Earle looked startled, then relieved.

"You're sure you don't want to tell your side?" he said. "The two of you could go into the Green Room."

Tess shook her head. The station had been good to her for many years, and she had no desire to hurt it out of spite. What could she accomplish except to look defensive, anyway?

"I'm sure," she said.

The reporter from Dayton started a protest, but Earle smiled briefly.

"In that case, maybe you'd better go help Heather," he said.

Chapter Twenty

FROM THE SIDELINES, TESS WATCHED THE LIGHTED SET of "Tess and Guests." The show was only halfway over, and Heather was floundering. The mother whose children had been snatched was drumming her fingers in anger and had just reacted to something Heather had said with such icy indignation that Tess expected her to rise and stalk off camera, leaving Heather high and dry in her crisp linen suit, which looked much too dressy for anyone's kitchen.

"But then you must know your children surely miss you as much as you miss them," said Heather. Her smile came so easily that anyone watching would know she didn't have any empathy for the problem.

Tess watched with only mild interest, one part of her baffled that she could feel so detached. The better part of her mind, however, was still back on the conversation with Albert. It only served to prove, she thought, how good Forrest truly was.

She thought she understood now. He had backed out of marriage because of some fear of mistreating children as he'd been mistreated—a misguided fear, surely. But why, then, had he been so angry when she withdrew herself and Zach from him? If he had meant—

But she didn't know what he had meant. Moreover, she was too weary, her spirits too low, to pursue the question. What difference did it make, anyway, she asked herself for the thousandth time? Zach needed a change of environment. Her first responsibility was to Zach; it was all as simple as that.

The studio lights were coming up. The show was over. Katie met her in the hall outside with a clap on the shoulder.

"How'd you like to go to lunch?" she inquired. "You, me, and Jack with a magnificent bottle of wine to celebrate your being free of this funny farm."

"Sounds good to me," said Tess, and minutes later they left.

When they got back, it was after one o'clock.

"So let them fire us next," said Katie under her breath.

"Tess wasn't fired. She went out in a blaze of glory," Jack reminded her.

He was in a fine mood from the wine, though Tess herself was stone sober. At least all the pickets were gone, as she herself would be in a short time along with her severance pay, she thought.

But as soon as Katie pushed the corral door open, Tess sensed some change in the atmosphere inside. More people were visiting in small groups than was normal at any one time. There was a steady buzz of conversation, a detectable excitement.

"Hey, here she is!" someone called.

Then, all at once, Tess found people around her. P. T. was hugging her and grinning. Ollie, the weatherman, was pumping her hand.

"Boy, lady, I'm glad to see you finally getting the support you ought to get," said a cameraman. "Congratulations!"

"For what?" asked Tess, bewildered.

"What's going on here, anyway?" demanded Jack.

"Telegrams," said P. T., choking with excitement. "A mountain of them from nice solid groups like Churchwomen United and the P.T.A. Planned Parenthood, Knights of Columbus, advocates of rights for the retarded—just look!"

On Tess's desk, yellow pages had appeared in a tidy stack. She took it in slowly.

"And phone calls," said the pudgy reporter, who now had been reduced to getting his own coffee. "There've been a million of them. It started before your show went off the air—as soon as people saw Heather and realized you'd really been replaced."

"Apparently those skunks at WPET had something about you for their editorial this morning, too," said Ollie. "Said it was a shame how you were being criticized at a time in your life when you deserved support."

Tess, in a daze, moved toward her desk. There was even a telegram from a homemakers' group sponsored by the county extension service and a note saying that a Weight Watchers chapter had called saying its members thought she did a fine job representing women's views and wanted her to stay.

"The best entertainment," said Matt Saxton with a grin, "was when the leader of some secretaries' group stormed in here on her lunch hour and buttonholed Earle to hand him a petition. She told him she'd never even seen your show because she *had* to work to help out with the family bills but that she and her membership found it pretty damn scary some group could come along and try to make anyone in her position look like a villain. 'For all their talk about values, they seem pretty short on compassion,' she told him. The old boy couldn't even get a word in edgewise."

Tess collapsed in her chair, still not sure what to make of this. Katie squeezed her shoulder.

"Well, looks like you're vindicated," she said.

A lot of good it does me, Tess thought. *Those people who've been attacking me may have to pull back now, but I've already quit my job; they've already torpedoed my life.*

She looked up and, through the glass window in Josh Jergens' office, saw Heather pacing, talking to him, arms folded in front of her. The leggy brunette came out and strode toward her desk, sparing a single, sullen look in Tess's direction.

"And," P. T. was saying, "the ad department has been getting calls all morning from people saying they'll pull their commercials if you do quit!"

A phone rang, distant yet at Tess's hand. Answering it, she found a stranger encouraging her to ignore small-minded criticism.

Tess felt something grow and crowd out her bitterness. The world had its share of people who were basically good, people who could shake off apathy and take a stand for fairness when the occasion demanded. Even if they barely outnumbered the stinkers, just knowing they were there made struggling worthwhile.

As she sat with the thoughts reeling through her mind, she saw Earle Lewis come out of his office and look at her. That was all, just that look, and then he disappeared again. What was he thinking?

The phone beside her rang again.

"Tess?" It was Earle's voice. "Would you come to my office?"

She went slowly, philosophically, gritting her teeth. There was, after all, nothing more he could do to her, was there?

When she stepped inside, Earle was on the phone. He hung up, his white-blond hair briefly shadowing his blue eyes before he sat back.

"Well," he said. "Heather didn't make a particularly good showing this morning, did she?"

He sounded dangerous. Antagonistic. Tess faced him with little interest.

"She'll get the knack of it quickly, I'm sure."

Did the words sound sarcastic? Tess didn't care.

"You've stirred up quite a storm," Earle said. "The biggest one this station's ever faced."

"By all appearances, it should be over in another day or two."

Earle started to speak again, then interrupted himself.

164

"Ah, Josh—Heather—come in and close the door."

Heather looked wary. She distanced herself from both men. She seemed angry with Josh and kept her attention on Earle.

The station manager put his lean brown fingers together.

"Well," he said mildly, "we seem to be experiencing quite a groundswell of support for Tess. As you may have heard, half a dozen ad accounts have threatened to cancel if we don't reinstate her."

He gave Tess a wry look. The silence was thick as his words ceased.

"We've become a classic case of how a small special-interest group can manipulate events," he continued. "Or at least a business once it starts to turn the screws. Might as well explore the phenomenon—air our dirty linen in the hopes that others might benefit. Tony's doing a feature on the subject for tonight's news.

"In view of what's happened, the people in advertising, along with the owners of this station, think Tess should stay. So do I, as a matter of fact. However, Heather's proved her skill at doing features, and I like to be fair. So I wanted to see you all together to see if we can't work this out.

"Tess, I gather you still like the early schedule since it allows you to be home when your child's done with school. We'll keep you on features four mornings a week, and of course you'll continue with "Tess and Guests" if all this is amenable to you.

"Heather, we'll let you do regular features for Saturday and Sunday evenings and for Wednesday morning, which we'll naturally trim from Tess's schedule. We'll cut you to half time on your public-service work. What do you say?"

Tess was stunned. Should she speak up? Say she wouldn't consider staying here now because she'd concluded Zach needed a change?

Heather didn't give her a chance.

"Work my tail off doing features for the two nights a week nobody watches the news, for the simple reason there is no real news?'' she asked, her voice rising in pitch. ''If that's the best you can do, then no, thanks!''

''I understand you're scheduled to do some sort of story this afternoon,'' Earle said, unperturbed. ''Of course we'll use that—''

But Heather swung on him.

''If you want your stupid feature, *you* go after it! Or send Little Mother here, since you think she's so great! I've had more than enough of this two-bit hick station. It's a joke. It's a graveyard. But no one who works here's even bright enough to see it. Even if you'd given me the job you promised me two days ago, I wouldn't have wasted more than another year of my time here. Now I don't plan to waste another five minutes!

''And you!'' She spun to face Josh now. ''I should have known you weren't even close to being the big man around here you thought you were! I should have known you wouldn't have spine enough to do anything for me when the going got rough! If I'd had any sense, I'd have thrown in with him from the first instead of you—I had the chance, you know!''

Like an angry child on the verge of tears, she flounced out the door.

Tess felt a stab of pity for Josh, who looked genuinely stricken.

''Heather!'' he croaked, his pipe nearly slipping from his teeth, and dashed out after her.

Earle watched calmly, as though none of this, not even Heather's last comment, affected him. Glancing at Tess, he raised an eyebrow.

''You know, Tess, I have to hand you this much. For a woman, you really are amazingly stable.''

Tess gave him a long look and knew she came dangerously close to detesting him. On the other hand, she now bore the smallest grain of grudging respect for him—about the same size as the one that had led him to offer what he must perceive as a compliment, she suspected. He did, as he'd said, try for a certain fairness. He'd made no attempt to keep her from talking to that reporter from the paper yesterday. And if he'd been set on getting rid of her, he could surely have found some way to keep from turning back in spite of these latest developments.

"Earle, I'm not at all sure I'm interested in coming back to work here," she said.

He winced dramatically, for her sake, she felt sure. His words, though, suggested he did indeed experience some visceral reaction.

"I suppose we need to talk money, don't we? Well, I've been authorized to offer a raise of a hundred a month."

It annoyed Tess he assumed that she was holding out for money.

"I wasn't angling for that," she said dryly. "But of course, since it's been offered, I'll expect it as part of the terms if I should say yes."

She started to leave, then paused and looked back.

"I'm afraid it will be several days before I give you an answer. A week, maybe. That leaves you in a bind here, I realize, what with Heather walking out, but I don't feel like being noble just now, and I need the time to think. You should know, too, that I've sent tapes to a couple of other stations. If they show interest, I'll be interviewing there. In the meantime, if you need to reach me, I'll be at home."

Her hand was on the doorknob when she heard Earle clear his throat.

"I hope you do decide to stay," he said.

Tess hesitated, then dipped her head in acknowledgment. Ignoring curious faces as she left the corral, she walked down the stairs and out of the station.

As the spring air hit her, she thought of Forrest. She thought of the afternoon when, unshaven and weary from his long hours in surgery, he'd taken her home. She thought of his introducing her to his friends, how proud he'd been. Yes, she'd been—what was Katie's word?—vindicated. She'd been vindicated, but now she was alone.

Chapter Twenty-One

THE HOUSE FELT EMPTY. SO DID TESS. EVEN WHEN Zach came home, alone but untormented, she was aware of a restlessness that would not leave. It was the letdown, she told herself, the reaction of nerves that no longer needed to be held tight.

"Guess what?" she said as she washed two apples at the kitchen sink and tossed one to Zach. "They've decided at work that they like the way I do my show just fine. In fact, they're even offering to pay me more money."

"That's nice," he said, but the words were the words of a child, with no real understanding. He peered listlessly at the apple. "You know it is pretty weird how this is all we ever have around and Forrest keeps good stuff."

"Sorry," she said, determined not to let the complaint get to her. "I'm not a very good cookie baker, and I guess I forget to buy them. For what it's worth, I do try to think about your teeth, too, you know." She paused. "There's some of that ice cream left. I guess you could have that."

The ice cream Forrest had brought, she meant, but for some reason she avoided saying his name.

Zach shook his head. "It's okay." The back door banged behind him as he went out to sit on the back step and listen to the other children playing.

Tess said an angry word beneath her breath and kicked a drawer shut. Sometimes it seemed Zach wasn't making any effort at all. Almost immediately, her thought was lost in guilt.

Come on, Tess, you're sore because he's not filling a role in your life you'd like him to fill, and that's not fair.

Maybe she should have stayed after work and talked with Katie. But then she wondered what difference talking would make. She had another decision to reach now, about staying at the station when she'd resigned herself to leaving, that was all. The phone rang, and she answered it with an eagerness that surprised her. It was Bill.

"What *is* this?" he asked as though taxed to the limit. "Radio, TV, papers—your name's on every one of them. *My* name, I might point out! When are you going to stop it?"

Tess looped the telephone cord around her finger. Once his words might have angered her. Now they merely seemed childish.

"As a matter of fact," she said, "since you asked, I'm thinking of moving. South Dakota or Oklahoma. How does that strike you?"

By the silence on the other end, she knew he was stunned.

"What would you *do?* I thought you'd had your fill of moving."

How like him not to suppose she could get a job anywhere else, Tess thought. But then she'd doubted the prospects of that herself at one time.

"I was tired of being dragged around as your appendage, yes. When it's a matter of my own work, I find it's different."

His voice grew harsh now, increasing in volume.

"See here, Tess, if this is your idea of a joke, it's not very funny! If you think you can just up and drag Zach away, let me remind you I have visitation rights!"

"Zach could spend time with you every summer. Two weeks, three—whatever it is, it would be more time than he gets to spend with you now. Meanwhile, are you by any chance calling to plan something with him? He's been begging.''

''Well, he's getting old enough to learn to live with disappointment. I'm getting ready to go out of town on business.''

''Fine. I'll give your regrets. When you get back, if you want to see Zach, call. Otherwise, Bill, please don't bother me with your opinions and tantrums about imagined damage to your good name. That goes for your mother, too. You can call if you want to make plans to see your son. Period.''

Tess banged the phone down and held it, knowing she was silly to feel that by the very force of her hand she kept Bill from calling back. Briefly, she felt a sense of introducing a welcome order into her life. Then she felt sorry for Zach, though she knew that really he'd lost nothing.

He has to know the truth about his father someday, she thought. *If only there were some way I could make Bill's lack of interest easier*. None came to mind as she stood there, however. Finally, exhausted by her day, she poured herself a glass of wine and went into the living room and sat down.

The last time she'd done that had been the day of the accident. With conscious effort, she closed her eyes, leaned back, and pushed the thought from her mind. They had to rediscover routine, both she and Zach. But as had happened so often today, she found her thoughts swinging back full circle to Forrest.

It's not too late, an inner voice whispered. You could go to him, make the first move. Women do that now. And surely Lucille misrepresented things with that story of hers. Yet the facts remained, clear and hanging in the silent air before her: Forrest had referred to her having a life *apart* from Zach. He also had raised the question of whether Zach's father might be interested in having custody of him. He had even, had he not, admitted to what Lucille said?

Cross, Tess rubbed her forehead, caught up by this

argument that raged within. *Damn it, I love Forrest, if such a thing's possible after just one week,* she acknowledged bitterly.

But she loved Zach, too. She had a commitment there. Only those with no ties, no conflicting loyalties, could indulge themselves in a totally selfish love.

The wine beside her was only half finished. Somehow, though, Tess found she had lost her taste for it. It reminded her of the cookout at Forrest's—of too many things. Returning to the kitchen, she poured the rest of it down the drain.

Needing some release, she prepared dinner with uncommon energy. She rolled chicken in corn-flake crumbs and made a cake—a real celebration. She put a candle in a silver saucer on the table, but Zach didn't notice. After they'd done the dishes, she read to him until she put him to bed.

"Mom?" he said as she was leaving the room, her finger poised to flip out the light. Once such a delaying tactic, because of its very frequency, would have provoked her. Now she turned back, eager for every small evidence of his reaching out.

"Yes, Zach?"

He peered at her over the covers. She could not really see his expression.

"You remember Billy? At Forrest's house? Do you think we could invite him over one of these days?"

She hadn't the least idea what Billy's last name was. And if they were going to move, anyway—

"Of course," she said.

In the archway into the living room, she rested one arm against the wall and sighed. Well, as usual, she'd worked herself into a corner. Either she'd grit her teeth and call Forrest to get the name of a child Zach would probably never see again if they moved, or she'd ignore this one small step of progress her son had made.

In his glass cage, Herman the hermit crab pulled himself into his coral-tinged shell and vanished, safe and presumably

171

happy in some dull-witted way. Suddenly, with a sense of amazement, Tess laughed.

"Good God," she said aloud. "I'm acting just like him!"

She stood still and let the unwelcome revelation seep through her.

Yes, it no doubt would be wise to leave this house. But didn't the rest of the changes she'd been contemplating amount to drawing away from dangers just as Herman did? Wouldn't it be opting for an existence not unlike his?

It took some fine and delicate talent to know whether you were suffering because you lacked gumption to run or whether the running itself was cowardice and proof you lacked the nerve to stick around and take a beating. She'd almost been too blinded by her own unhappiness, her own fears, to recognize that difference.

It *would* be easier starting over in some other town, easier not encountering people who knew about Zach's accident, easier not running into Lucille or having to deal with the constant upsets caused by Bill. But was that the kind of person she wanted to be? Was that the kind of example she wanted to set for Zach? If there had been people who turned against her here, there also had been total strangers, with no ax to grind and no special interest to protect, who had voiced support of her. If she'd had adversaries at the studio, she'd also had friends.

Maybe it had looked easier running from Forrest, too, she admitted, sinking into a chair. Certainly it was less painful to believe things wouldn't work out than to hope they would, only to see them fail—far less painful to tell yourself you'd been a fool and pull out relatively intact than to let yourself in for what might prove to be only a brief affair, with Zach and Lucille and dozens of others on hand to witness your folly.

But damn it, did she want to live her life like that hermit crab? Tess buried her face in her hands.

She didn't want to think about this. She deserved a break, surely, after what she'd been through.

A lot of people deserved them, her conscience told her. But maybe there *were* no breaks. Maybe you created your own. Or maybe it was a matter of seizing them, of facing up to opportunities when they came.

For a moment, she sat very still, feeling more reckless than she ever had before in her life. With a breath, she gathered herself and went to the telephone, thinking how absurd it was she did not even know the number. What if it was unlisted? What if—

"Forrest?" she said breathlessly as he answered. "It's Tess."

She did not know what ought to come next. It flashed through her mind that the station might withdraw the offer of a contract she'd been so cool to today. And this call might lead nowhere or only to difficult choices between her own pleasure and duty to Zach. But what kind of a life could you lead if you were always so afraid of blows that you never stuck your neck out?

"I behaved like a coward the other night when you came by and tried to talk," she said. "But I'm not. I don't think. So I'm calling to—to—"

"Has Albert been talking to you?" he interrupted. The words were flat.

"Yes. He—he called this morning." She knew she was floundering. "Forrest, don't hang up! Please listen. I think you're damn lucky to have Albert, but nothing he said made me change my mind. It's just that I've finally managed to think things through and—

"Look, I know I'm bungling this. I'm not saying what I mean. I'm scared, putting myself out on a limb like this. I don't even know whether you care enough to—want to talk about this."

The line was so silent she thought he had hung up already.

"Why don't I stop by?" he said at last.

While she waited, Tess tried to force shape on her thoughts and could not. Forrest had sounded wary, not like his old self. When the doorbell rang, her fingers shook so, she could hardly unfasten the night chain.

"Zach asleep?" he asked, standing outside.

Tess nodded. He stepped over the threshold, and suddenly she was more than ever at a loss for words.

"I'm sorry," she said.

He inclined his head as though that were enough for starters. Tess knew she must have felt pain, some feeling of loss, when Bill left. But it was nothing compared with the sharpness of what she was feeling now. Seeing Forrest, so large and solemn, she was overpowered by a desire to feel his arms encircle her. The hope that she might, and the alternate dread that she never would, beat at her ears until she could scarcely hear.

Like two people awaiting attack, they walked separately into the living room. Forrest sat stiffly in the chair, which was usually hers.

"That was quite an interesting article on the group that was picketing in the paper tonight," he said. "It's apparently caused quite a backlash. So where does that leave your status with the station? Are you staying?"

"I've decided to, yes. I'm going to put this house on the market because I think Zach would do better somewhere else, but—" Breaking off, she took a breath. "I don't want you to think I called just because I'm staying. The two aren't really related. I'd be staying whether—whether you'd been willing to talk to me or not. I'd have said what I'm trying to say, somehow, even if I'd gone."

He said nothing, merely looked at her, and after a moment, Tess was forced to look away with withering spirits. This had all been for nothing. Albert had been wrong. Or she had. Or perhaps the wounds she'd inflicted the last time they'd met had simply been too deep, their relationship too new and tenuous to pick up again.

"Would you like some wine?" she asked, because, for the moment, it gave her something to do. She had gotten through the civilized motions of dealing with an ex-husband; she supposed she could get through this.

"I need something," he said, so cheerlessly it left her no hope.

In the kitchen, Tess got glasses out without seeing them. She lifted the three-liter jug that was her whole wine cellar, but her hand shook, splashing the counter with bright chianti.

"Here. Let me," said Forrest behind her, and she turned, startled. He took the jug, held it a moment, and the next thing Tess knew, their mouths were meeting.

Forrest's hands held her shoulders tightly, almost crushing them. They kissed as she had never kissed before in her life. All that she felt she tried to communicate without words.

"Oh, Tess—I've missed you, Tess—I love you—" Forrest held her away from him and scowled at her fiercely. "Did you hear that, Tess? I love you, and I'm not going to let you go."

She could scarcely breathe, let alone think, yet she knew that whatever might happen, just now nothing mattered but this.

"I—love you." Her words were halting.

"Then be honest with me. It wasn't just because of the need of a job you were set to slip away from me, was it?"

"No."

Holding more tightly to the soft folds of his shirt, Tess started to speak. He gave her no chance.

"It had something to do with that fiasco of mine with Dacia, didn't it? What were you told about that? Who told you?"

Tess knew before she said it how unfair she'd been. Yet she looked directly into his eyes as she answered and fought back the impulse to flinch.

"Lucille."

"And you were willing to believe her instead of me? You were willing to wave me aside without ever hearing what I might have to say?" He was angry and bitter. He shook her slightly. "Well, damn it, weren't you, Tess?"

"Yes."

She was ashamed now of the admission, but she faced it squarely. The only hope for anything between them lay in honesty.

His temper faded as quickly as it had flared. He pulled her against him.

"Tess, sweetheart, I'm sorry. I'm being a bully, and you've already been through enough."

She held him tightly. "No. You're absolutely right."

"I should have told you. But we'd known each other such a short time, and yes, I suppose I was afraid it might make me look bad in your eyes. I don't like to seem to justify myself in the business with Dacia. But then I don't like the way I appear to have come off in all this, either."

Pausing, he kissed her briefly, then draped one arm on top of the refrigerator, looking down at her.

"All right, you know the rudiments of the story from Lucille, I gather. What's missing is this. I'd dated that woman for six months and didn't know children existed. They didn't live with her. She'd farmed them out to her parents. I stumbled over them almost literally."

Suddenly, Tess knew what Lucille had told her about the suggestion of boarding school had been a lie.

"It—didn't have anything to do with you not wanting to be around children, then?"

He shook his head.

"It just seemed to me a relationship that short on openness didn't have a damn thing going for it."

Closing her eyes, Tess sighed.

"Albert told me about the two of you being mistreated when you were children," she said carefully.

Even though they weren't touching, she could feel him stiffen and start to draw away. Opening her eyes, she caught his hand and held it firmly. After several seconds, his fingers loosened. They curled around hers.

"He thinks that had something to do with your decision," Tess said. "That you had some fear of repeating the cycle or something."

His smile was strained.

"Al's usually right on target, but he missed by a mile on that one. But Tess—" He lowered his gaze, which was dark and brooding. "I do have a problem of some sort. I can't seem to handle physical contact—at least not with kids. I'm sure you must have noticed it with Zach."

He let his breath out as though admitting it were a great relief.

"I don't know why. I expect maybe Al could tell me. At my office, in my chair, I see kids sometimes, and that's okay. I poke in their mouths and rearrange their chins, and it's no problem. But I can't—I'm crazy about Zach. There've been half a dozen times when I thought I couldn't stand it not to scoop him up and tell him things would be okay or turn him upside down and try to coax a giggle out of him or something. But I can't. And when he's touched me, you've seen what's happened."

Her fingers hurt now, he was holding them so tightly. With her free hand, Tess reached up and touched his face.

"You're good," she said softly. "You're totally good and gentle, and I know that. But yes, I'd noticed—and you'd said I needed a life *apart* from Zach, which I realize now probably just meant doing what I wanted sometimes. You'd also asked about Bill showing interest in having custody of Zach, though. So when Lucille said you'd walked out because of children I—it frightened me. I think I was already worried. No, I was terrified! I was starting to realize just how deeply I felt about you."

And I didn't know where it would lead, she finished silently. *I still don't.* She looked at him, overcome now by her own uncertainty.

"Oh, Tess." He smoothed back her hair as she sometimes smoothed Zach's. His smile was wrinkling through again. "I asked about the custody because Zach's father strikes me as a first-class bastard, not to mention a troublemaker. It occurred to me that if you and I had any sort of affair and he had evidence, he might try to take Zach away."

He might, thought Tess. *Bill's just that kind.*

"I'll have to chance it," she said, raising her mouth for the kiss they both had been needing too long.

In the warm pressure of his arms, she felt assurance that everything she'd done tonight, every decision that she had made, had been to the good. They lost themselves in the need for each other, touching, caressing. Their bodies strained against each other as Forrest buried his hands in the depths of her hair.

Tess's breathing had quickened. She felt a wild, leaping desire. Forrest broke a hard kiss and looked into her eyes.

"Can I stay, Tess? I know it's not good, what with Zach here. But I don't want to go. I need you tonight."

"I need *you!*" Tess kissed him violently. Something special bound them—knowledge of the comfort and the healing they could give each other.

So if it feels right, let's move on it.

Forrest had said that so long ago, it seemed. Now she understood. Now she knew he'd been right. She sighed as he parted her lips, claiming her completely, and lifted her into his arms.

"I'll be up and gone before you wake Zach."

Tess nodded.

Always, she thought, there was the desire to have things tied up in neat packages, to have some hope that what lay ahead might be more lasting than an occasional stolen night together. For her, for many women, she suspected, there was the hunger for commitment or for promises.

Only promises were easily broken. She'd known that for a long time. So what was the point, then, in worrying where the future led?

Chapter Twenty-Two

TESS LAY AGAINST THE SOLIDNESS OF THE MAN SHE loved best in all the world. He was sleeping peacefully. Drowsy, she wondered what had roused her from her own contentment, and for the briefest instant, fear brushed its wings over her. She was so happy now, but what if it didn't last?

With a yawn, she informed her old nemesis she didn't care. Burrowing closer to Forrest in the predawn darkness, she curled one arm across his naked chest.

"Mom?"

Zach's voice spoke to her, close at hand. With a gasp, Tess came fully awake to realize the bedroom door was standing open. Surely she could not have failed to hear her alarm go off—no, Zach had awakened and come in search of her as he had that other time since Andy's death.

"Zach—" Her voice was hoarse as she tried to make the inevitable situation keep from happening. But it was too late. He was staring at Forrest and at her.

"Oh," he said awkwardly. Confusion showed on his face, even in the darkness. "Never mind. It's okay." He began to back out of the room.

"Zach!" She tried to untangle herself from the sheets and find her robe. Beside her, Forrest stirred and reached for her.

"Tess?"

"It's Zach." She forced the words out. "He woke up and came in hunting me."

"Tess, wait!" Still groggy with sleep, he struggled to catch her, but Tess dashed out.

Damn it, why hadn't she thought of this possibility? She'd felt so confident last night, thought she had every aspect of her life under control. But she'd been deluding herself, hadn't she? she demanded angrily. Oh, she knew the decisions she'd made were right for her, but how was she going to explain them to her son?

She peered into his room. He wasn't there. A sound of movement came to her from the kitchen. Fumbling with the belt to her robe, which refused to tie, she found him there.

He was kneeling on the kitchen counter, his back toward her. A cupboard door was open, and Zach had a glass in his hand.

"I guess I woke up because I was hungry—or something," he said as he saw her. "I'm going to get a glass of milk. Okay?"

He slid from the counter and started past her, his eyes downcast. Tess caught at his shoulder.

"Zach. Let me try to explain. I know you must be— disappointed with me."

He squirmed uncomfortably, but he turned back.

"Come on, Mom. I'm not a dumb little five-year-old. I know grownups do it." He paused, and a small frown crossed his face. "I don't understand quite why, except to make babies, but I know they do."

He slipped from her grasp and continued to the refrigerator. Tess could almost hear his mind working as he got out the milk, then looked at her again.

"Anyway, it's no different from Dad and Caroline, is it? It's no big deal."

It's very different from your father and Caroline, Tess wanted to say. Only she couldn't think of a single explanation of how it was. She sat down in a chair before her knees could collapse.

She started to speak, but a sound in the doorway behind her made her turn. Forrest stood there, barefoot, clad only in slacks, his bare chest very large and very male. His hair was rumpled, and he blinked in the bright light of the kitchen. He looked out of place there. An intruder. Yet it seemed right, too, as he calmly inserted himself in their small family group.

"You're up mighty early, Zach," he said, turning a chair around and straddling it.

Zach measured him with his eyes. "I got hungry."

"Yeah? That happens to me sometimes."

Forrest poured milk into Zach's already-empty glass and drained it. Zach watched him.

Tess thought of the night Forrest had tried to carry the sleeping boy into the house. Zach had been angry. 'He's not my father!' Zach had objected. Would that same resentment surface now?

"I hope you don't mind too much finding me here," said Forrest easily. "I'm sure it's not the best of surprises. But the fact is, Zach, I'm hoping to marry your mother. If she'll have me, that is—if you will."

He glanced at her then, and Tess knew he must have seen the answer written on her face. He started to smile.

"Oh, Forrest—" Her voice broke. "This isn't just because of—" She couldn't finish, couldn't put into words the fear that this might be only a noble gesture, designed to keep her from shame in her child's eyes.

"It's because we didn't get as far as talking about all the details last night."

Tess looked at the open wine jug still on the counter and knew what he meant. Reaching out, she took his hand.

But Zach had not responded at all. When Forrest's voice once more broke the silence, the edges were sharp.

"Zach. Come around here, please."

Swiveling around the right way in his chair, Forrest swallowed deeply. As Zach approached, he reached awkwardly out, and with face gone white but firmly set, pulled the boy onto his lap.

"I love you, Zach. I want you to know that. But I'm not very good at showing it. I'm not good at hugging and things because—my dad never did it with me.

"I may never be good at those things, Zach. And I know I'll never be able to take your father's place; I'd never try. All I can promise is that I'll always be your friend. And that I'll be here when you need me—always."

Zach began to cry softly. Tess's breath faltered as she saw him reach forward, aiming his face toward the sheltering security of Forrest's chest. A second on which all their destinies seemed to ride fluttered past. But already they were locked together, man and boy, Forrest's arms around Zach and his cheek bent, as though it were the most natural thing in the world, against Zach's head.

"Nobody wants to be my friend," said Zach, the words at last choked out of him. "Why would you?"

"Because I like you. Because I know lots of people before you have made mistakes they're sorry for and they're still fine people—just as you are. And I guess maybe it's because I'm lonesome, too."

Zach sat up, his face wet, and wiped it on his pajama sleeve.

"When?" he said. "Were you thinking of marrying Mom, I mean?"

"If we got the license today, we could get married Monday. I guess that's what I'd like to do. I feel like this is a pretty bad time in your lives, and I'd like to be with you. Full-time. I'd like to take care of you."

For the first time since he'd pulled Zach onto his lap, Forrest sent Tess a hesitant look. She felt so full of joy, of love for both of them, that she wanted to reach out in a quick embrace, only the moment seemed somehow too special for movement.

"If we got the license today," said Zach, "would that mean we could get the dog on Monday, too?"

"Dog? What dog?"

Forrest's look was so blank that Tess began to laugh at how he'd fallen into this trap of his own creation.

"Oh, *that* dog," he said. "Uh—yes. I think the waiting period's the same for dogs."

He stood up, juggling Zach easily to one arm. Tess, unable to restrain herself, hugged them both, crying and laughing.

"Hey," she said, feeling this last small victory she pushed for was vital. "You both say you're hungry, and I've heard ladies about to be married don't cook. What say we all get dressed and go to the pancake house?"

She saw Zach swallow, much as Forrest had. He reached out to clutch a fold of her robe as though he needed to feel himself connected to both of them.

"I don't deserve it," he said in a low voice. "Andy liked pancakes, too, and he'll never get to have them again—not ever."

Tess felt her heart give a hard, explosive beat, nearly splitting her chest. So much depended on this. So much depended on things she herself was only now learning.

"Zach, one of the things about life—one of the things that makes all the bad times worthwhile—is that sometimes we all get things we don't deserve."

She thought of Forrest.

"Wonderful things, Zach. Sometimes big and sometimes little, like having pancakes. We've got to take those good things. We were meant to."

Forrest's fingers pressed hers gently. They both watched Zach.

He was silent so long Tess thought she couldn't bear it. Then a huge sigh escaped him as though he had considered and decided to close some inner door behind him.

"Forrest looks like he's pretty hungry. Yeah, let's go there."

With a childlike shrewdness Tess had almost forgotten he possessed, he turned to the man who was holding him.

"Hey, will it really rot my teeth like she always says if I have chocolate milk?"

ATTENTION ROMANCE FANS!

If you enjoyed this book and would like to receive a free subscription to Ballantine's Love & Life Romance Newsletter, fill out the coupon below. You'll get personal glimpses into romance authors' lives and work, and more news of new and unforgettable romantic reading from Ballantine.

LOVE & LIFE

Romance
Newsletter
for the woman who wants the most from love & life.

BALLANTINE BOOKS, Dept. Love & Life
201 E. 50th Street, New York, N.Y. 10022

Yes, please send me a free subscription to Ballantine's Love & Life Romance Newsletter.

Name_____

Address_____

City_____State_____Zip Code_____

Dear Reader:

Your opinions are important to us so please take a few moments to tell us your thoughts. It will help us give you more enjoyable LOVE & LIFE Books in the future.

1. Where did you obtain this book?

				5
Bookstore	☐ 1	Newsstand	☐ 6	
Supermarket	☐ 2	Airport	☐ 7	
Variety/discount store	☐ 3	From A Friend	☐ 8	
Department store	☐ 4	Other_____		
Drug store	☐ 5	(write in)		

2. On an overall basis, how would you rate this book?

Excellent ☐ 1   Good ☐ 3   Poor ☐ 5   6
Very Good ☐ 2   Fair ☐ 4

3. What did you like best about this book?

Heroine ☐ 1 Hero ☐ 2 Setting ☐ 3 Story line ☐ 4   7
Love scenes ☐ 5 Ending ☐ 6 Other Characters ☐ 7

4. Do you prefer love scenes that are

Less explicit than   More explicit than
  in this book ☐ 1   in this book ☐ 2   8
       About as explicit as in this book ☐ 3

5. How likely would you be to purchase other LOVE & LIFE Editions in the future?

Extremely likely ☐ 1   Not very likely ☐ 3   9
Somewhat likely ☐ 2   Not at all likely ☐ 4

6. Please indicate your age group.

Under 18 ☐ 1   25–34 ☐ 3   50 or older ☐ 5   10
18–24 ☐ 2   35–49 ☐ 4

If you would like a free subscription to the LOVE & LIFE Romance Newsletter, please fill in your name and address.

NAME_____

ADDRESS_____

CITY_____STATE_____ZIP CODE_____   11

Please mail to: Ballantine Books
                 LOVE & LIFE Research Dept.
                 516 Fifth Avenue—Suite 606
                 New York, N.Y. 10036

L-11

MORE WONDERFUL STORIES FROM

LOVE & LIFE

The Best Man
by Carole Nelson Douglas

What do you do if you discover your husband is gay?
Barbara Collins, a prosecuting attorney in St. Paul Min-
nesota, marries dashing state senator Elliot Randolph and
expects to live happily ever after. There are two things
she doesn't count on: Elliot's homosexuality and her own
growing feelings for his campaign manager, Jack Reese . . .

Separate Ways
by Fiona Harrowe

Though a married couple can grow together, they can
also grow apart. Elise Thompson and her husband Peter
have spent many years traveling all over the world
together. Now, after completing her law degree, she's found
a job in San Diego and wants to settle down. But Peter's
wanderlust hasn't ceased—and it propels her into the arms
of an older man . . .

On Sale June 1983